SOPHIE AND THE ALBINO CAMEL

Sophie
and the
Albino Camel

STEPHEN DAVIES

ILLUSTRATED BY DAVE SHELTON

ANDERSEN PRESS
LONDON

First published in 2006 by
Andersen Press Limited,
20 Vauxhall Bridge Road, London SWIV 2SA
www.andersenpress.co.uk

British Library Cataloguing in Publication Data available

ISBN-10: 1 84270 551 2
ISBN-13: 978 1 84270 551 3

Typeset by FiSH Books, Enfield, Middx.
Printed and bound in Great Britain by Bookmarque Ltd.,
Croydon, Surrey

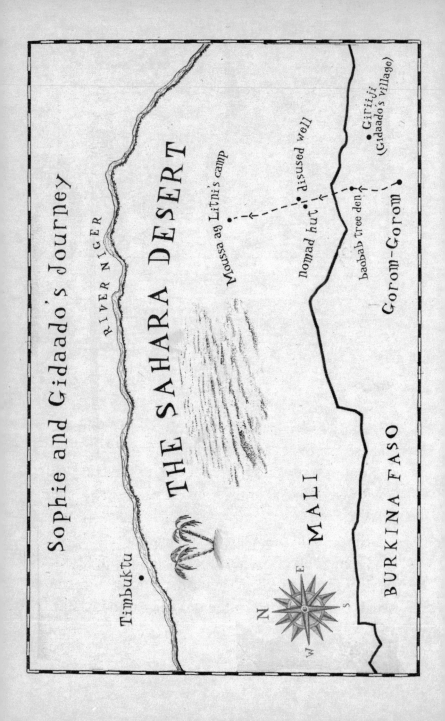

Sophie and Gidaado's Journey

RIVER NIGER

THE SAHARA DESERT

Timbuktu

MALI

BURKINA FASO

Moussa ag Litni's camp

disused well

nomad hut

baobab tree den

Gorom-Gorom

Giriiji
(Gidaado's village)

N E S W

Chapter 1

'Seventy-five francs,' said the fat woman. 'These are the sweetest bananas in Africa.'

Sophie screwed up her face as if she had just swallowed a Saharan sand-slug. 'Forty,' she said.

'Sixty,' said the woman, 'and not a franc less.'

Sophie delved in her pocket and brought out a fifty-franc piece. When she held it up, the small coin gleamed in the dazzling midday sun.

The woman clicked her tongue in disgust. 'Sixty,' she said.

Sophie smiled sweetly at her and began to walk away. One step, two steps, three steps...

'All right!' called the woman. 'Fifty francs, and may God have mercy on you.'

Sophie bought the bunch of bananas, and headed for the charmer's stall. She knew her way around Gorom-Gorom market easily by now. She and her dad had lived in Gorom-Gorom for two years, and she could speak Fulfulde almost as well as the locals.

There was a crowd of people at the charmer's stall and Sophie had to push her way to the front. The charmer, Salif dan Bari, was in full flow. Wrapped around his head was a long green turban, and wrapped around his arm was a long green snake. The snake glared at Sophie with its narrow yellow eyes. Its forked tongue flickered towards her and it hissed. Sophie grinned back at it. She had seen this act too many times to be afraid.

'Meet Mamadou the rope,' said Salif dan Bari, 'the deadliest creature in Africa.'

No one here called a snake a snake. People thought that if you said the word 'snake', the nearest snake would think you were calling it and would come looking for you. So they always said 'rope' instead.

'One bite from Mamadou and you would be dead within three minutes,' said the charmer.

'*Oooh*,' said the crowd, stepping back.

Right on cue the snake reared up and bit Salif dan Bari on the nose. '*Aargh*!' he yelled.

'*Oooh*,' said the crowd again, enjoying themselves immensely.

'*Zorki!*' cried the charmer. 'I've been bitten on the nose by a deadly green rope! What shall I do?'

'Take a Salif rope pill!' yelled a small girl. Sophie recognised the girl from school, but she was not a particular friend of hers. In fact, Sophie did not have any real friends in Gorom-Gorom. Even though she could now speak Fulfulde well, the children at school still kept their distance from her. She knew why, of course. The local children had all grown up together and knew everything about each other. She was a stranger here; she was the weird and wonderful white girl who spoke with a funny accent and drank filtered water from a plastic bottle. Dad was no help; he was always telling her to make some friends, but it was easier said than done.

'A Salif rope pill,' continued the charmer, holding up a tiny blue tablet. 'Good idea.' He began to sing:

'A rope has nipped you on the nose?
One Salif rope pill will end your woes.
An angry rope attacked your wife?
One Salif rope pill could save her life.'

Salif dan Bari popped the blue tablet into his mouth and sighed. 'Mmmm, I feel better already,' he said.

'Maybe that is because Mamadou the rope has no poison fangs,' shouted someone at the back of the crowd, and everyone laughed.

It was true and they all knew it – Mamadou the rope was fangless and the charmer was a conman. The people of Gorom-Gorom bought Salif rope pills not because they thought the pills were any good but because they enjoyed Salif's show.

*

Sophie continued walking. She enjoyed drinking in the sights and sounds of the market – the brightly coloured robes and headscarves of the women, the baskets of guavas and pawpaws, the huge white pyramids of grain, the cries of tradesmen and children, and the clatter of donkey carts.

Her next stop was the animal park, an area of sand by the lake where people parked their animals. There were clusters of donkeys and a long row of camels, all waiting patiently for their owners to return. Sophie liked the way the donkeys stood in twos, resting their heads on each other's backs. None of *them* was lonely, she thought.

The camels were kneeling in a row, facing the sun. Some of them seemed to be dozing. The animal park attendant was sitting nearby and he also seemed to be dozing.

'Wake up,' cried a short man in a glittery robe, kicking the attendant in the ribs. 'There have been six camels stolen in this area in the last month, and you sit there snoring your head off.'

'I was *pretending* to be asleep,' said the attendant indignantly. 'Lulls the thieves into a false sense of security.'

Then Sophie saw it. At the end of the row was a camel which was white from head to hump to hooves. There were lots of normal brownish camels but then this beautiful white one. She looked at its face. Usually camels look like they are smirking, but this one didn't. It looked serious, maybe even a little sad. It turned its big brown eyes towards Sophie and gazed at her from under half-closed eyelids. Its eyelashes were very long.

'*Salam alaykum*,' said a voice behind her.

Sophie spun round and saw a small boy. He was wearing baggy trousers with patches on both knees, and a yellow shirt with sleeves far too long for him. He was leaning on a long staff and grinning at her.

'*Alaykum asalam*,' said Sophie.

'Ugly, isn't he?' said the boy.

'No, I think he's beautiful,' said Sophie. 'I've never seen a white camel before.'

'And he's never seen a white girl before,' said

the boy. The boy's head was shaved completely bald and his front teeth stuck out a little. He looked friendly.

'What is his name?' asked Sophie.

'Chobbal,' said the boy. Chobbal was a kind of African food – a spicy rice pudding which Sophie did not like very much.

'I've never seen you at Gorom-Gorom school,' said Sophie.

'I don't go. I am a griot.'

Sophie had heard of griots but never met one. Griots were professional storytellers so they knew thousands of stories, riddles and songs. They were experts in African history, too – a good griot could remember the names and adventures of all the warriors and chiefs of his region during the past five hundred years. Whenever there was an important party, a baby's naming ceremony for example, the host of the party would hire a griot to come and sing for the guests. On these occasions the griot's songs were usually about how brave and wise and good-looking the host's ancestors all were.

'Do you want to hear my *tarik*?' said the boy.

'Okay,' said Sophie, not understanding the word.

The boy raised his arms and took a deep breath in, until his whole body seemed to swell up. Then he started to sing in a high-pitched wail:

> *'Hail, my name is Gidaado the Fourth*
> *Gidaado the son of Alu*
> *Alu son of Hamadou*
> *Hamadou son of Yero*
> *Yero son of Tijani*
> *Tijani son of—'*

'Okay,' said Sophie. 'That's enough I think.'

> *' – Haroun son of Gidaado the Third*
> *Gidaado the Third son of Salif*
> *Salif son of Ali*
> *Ali son of Gorko Bobo—'*

'Stop,' said Sophie.

> *'Gorko Bobo son of Adama*
> *Adama son of Hussein the Tall*

8

Hussein the Tall son of Gid – OUCH!'

'Sorry,' said Sophie, letting go of Gidaado the Fourth's ear.

Gidaado rubbed his ear and scowled. 'What's your name?' he said.

'Sophie,' said Sophie.

'Nice to meet you,' said Gidaado. 'I think.'

'Likewise,' said Sophie.

There was a sound of snoring from behind them. The animal park attendant had fallen asleep again.

'I should be heading back to my village,' said Gidaado.

'Okay,' said Sophie.

'Tell me something, Sofa,' said Gidaado, his face slowly breaking into a grin. 'Would you like a ride on Chobbal?'

Sophie looked at the beautiful white camel and then at Gidaado. Say 'no' to strangers, her dad had always told her. But hadn't he also told her to try and make some friends?

'All right,' said Sophie.

Chapter 2

Chobbal the camel swayed back and forth as he walked, and Sophie held onto the reins tightly. She had sat on a camel before but never gone as far as this. They were out of Gorom-Gorom now, and all around them were the flat sands of the Sahara, dotted here and there with little acacia bushes.

Sophie was worried. She was on the edge of one of the biggest deserts in the world and in her shoulder bag she had only a bottle of water and a bunch of bananas. Not only that but her travelling companion was a strange boy called Gidaado who didn't even go to school. He had said it was not far to his village but already they had been travelling for two hours.

What would Dad say if he could see her now? Would his glasses steam up, like they usually did when he was angry? Would he shout? Would he give her that lecture about Fatimata Tamboura getting lost in the Sahara? She had ended up having to chew acacia roots to survive, poor girl. 'Never mess with the Sahara Desert,' her dad often said.

Then again, maybe Dad would not be angry. These last few days he had been completely engrossed in his experiments on carnivorous plants of the desert. When Sophie had left the house that morning, Dad had been standing next to his desert flytrap, dangling a sand-slug above it.

'I'm going to the market,' she had said.

'Thanks, love,' he had replied, not looking up. 'Milk, two sugars, please.'

*

No, her dad was not like other parents. So long as Sophie was home by bedtime, he might not even realise that his daughter had been away.

Sophie sat in the saddle with her feet resting lightly in the U of the white camel's neck. Gidaado was perched precariously behind her on the back edge of the hump. Since they had left Gorom he had not stopped chattering.

'I have had Chobbal since he was a calf,' he was saying. 'When he was born, his own mother refused to give him milk, because he was so funny-looking. I had to give him milk every day from a calabash.'

Sophie thought of the calabashes at home that Dad studied. A calabash was a big round fruit, a bit like a watermelon but with a very hard shell. Calabashes were not at all nice to eat, but if you cut one in half and scooped all the insides out, the empty shells made great bowls for keeping milk or grain in. They made good drums, too.

'He's a fine camel,' said Gidaado. 'Look at those big strong teeth.'

Sophie did not fancy trying to look at

Chobbal's teeth whilst riding on his back. 'I'll take your word for it,' she said.

'Fast, too,' Gidaado went on. 'I'm thinking of entering him in the Oudalan Province Camel Race this year.' He whirled the wooden staff round and round in his hand and cried, '*Hoosh-ka!*'

The camel started to trot, then gallop, faster and faster. Sophie shrieked and doubled her grip on the reins. Chobbal lurched wildly as he ran, rocking from side to side, spit flying out of the sides of his mouth. Sophie bounced up and down on the saddle like a cowgirl in a rodeo.

'Stop him!' she shouted. 'I'm going to throw up!'

'What's that, Sofa?' shouted Gidaado. 'You want to speed *up*, you say? HOOSH-BARAKAAA!'

The camel lowered its head and strained forward, its hooves pounding the sand so hard that great clouds of dust flew up behind. The Saharan air blasting in Sophie's face felt like an enormous hairdryer pointed straight at her. She could hardly breathe. Her knuckles turned white as she gripped the upright wooden prong which formed the front of the saddle. The bananas in her shoulder bag flew out of the bag and out of sight.

'BANANAS OVERBOARD!' yelled Sophie. 'STOP!'

'*Bahaat-ugh!*' cried Gidaado. Straight away Chobbal lifted his head and began to slow down.

'I'll get you for that, Gidaado,' said Sophie, as Chobbal slowed to a walk. 'Turn him around and we'll fetch my bananas.'

'You turn him around, you're the one with the reins,' said Gidaado, grinning at her.

Sophie scowled and tugged the reins to one side. Chobbal looked round and raised an eyebrow.

'Be gentle with him, Sofa,' said Gidaado.

'My name is Sophie,' said Sophie.

Ten minutes later they were back on track. The sun was not so strong now, and there was a slight breeze.

'Tijani, my great-great-grandfather, was a camel racer,' said Gidaado, peeling a banana. 'He won the Oudalan Province Camel Race three times with Mad Mariama.'

'Mad Mariama?' said Sophie, laughing.

'Never was there a camel so utterly barmy. She bit off two of my great-great-grandfather Tijani's fingers.'

'Eew, that's gross.'

'Yes, well, Tijani wasn't thrilled about it, either. But Mad Mariama was the fastest camel in Oudalan so he put up with her bad behaviour. He got a gold nugget for each race Mad Mariama won. He entered her in the Oudalan Province "Pouring Tea From the Hump of a Camel" Competition as well but she was no good for that. Far too twitchy.'

'I can imagine,' said Sophie. She had seen people in Gorom-Gorom practising for that competition; it required a very steady hand and a very calm camel.

'Nice bananas,' said Gidaado.

Sophie gave him another, and took one for herself too. 'Tell me something,' she said. 'That man at Gorom-Gorom market said that six camels have been stolen in this area recently. Is that true?'

'Yes.'

'Who do people think the thief is?'

Gidaado looked around him and then leant forward and whispered in Sophie's ear, 'The thief is Moussa ag Litni.'

'Who is he?' whispered Sophie.

'A Tuareg bandit,' whispered Gidaado.

'We're in the middle of the desert,' whispered Sophie, 'so why are we whispering?'

'Sand has ears,' whispered Gidaado, and looked around him again.

Is he putting it on, thought Sophie to herself, or is he genuinely scared? 'Tell me about Moussa ag Litni,' she said.

'Okay,' said Gidaado, 'but don't blame me if it gives you nightmares.'

'It won't,' said Sophie.

Chapter 3

'Moussa ag Litni,' said Gidaado, 'is a Tuareg bandit chief. You know who the Tuaregs are, yes?'

'No,' said Sophie.

'What do they teach you at school? I thought you schoolchildren were supposed to know things. The Tuaregs are an ancient nomadic tribe, the lords of the Sahara Desert. They are sometimes called "the blue men of the desert" because they wear turbans of rich indigo cloth which dye their skin blue. They live in tents and keep camels, and they use the camels for travelling in the desert. With me so far?'

'Yes.'

'In the old days the people who lived south of the desert mined gold and the people north of the desert mined salt, and the Tuaregs used their camels to carry the salt across the desert. There was a city called Timbuktu where they used to exchange salt for gold. One kilogram of salt for one kilogram of gold, they say.'

As the sun sank lower in the sky, it turned a brilliant orange and the whole landscape around them was infused with a rich golden glow. This was always Sophie's favourite time of the day – the twenty golden minutes before dusk.

'I'd rather have a kilogram of gold than a kilogram of salt any day,' said Sophie.

'But the people south of the desert wanted salt to make their food taste good,' said Gidaado. 'You can't put gold on your chobbal, can you?'

'True,' said Sophie. 'And women can't hang salt on their ears.'

'Which is why they traded it. My great-great-great-great-great-great-great-grandfather Gorko Bobo used to visit Timbuktu regularly. It's only two weeks' ride from here if you have a decent camel. There is an ancient legend that the streets of Timbuktu were paved with gold, and in the centre of the city there was a huge pillar of gold which the Tuareg traders used to tie their camels to. It was the richest city in the world. Ask me if it is still like that.'

'Is it still like that?'

'No. Today Timbuktu is just a small desert town full of sand and postcard-salesmen. And griots, of course, singing their songs about the good old days.'

'Why did it change?'

'Salt is much less valuable than it used to be. These days we don't need salt to be carried across the desert by a caravan of Tuareg camels. We just buy it cheap from abroad. So ask me what the Tuaregs do now.'

'What do the Tuaregs do now?'

'Some of them make cushions out of leather. Some of them make knives and earrings out of silver. And others buy and sell camels.'

'And what does Moussa ag Litni do?'

'He buys and sells camels. Or rather, he *steals* and sells camels. There is a song that the griots in Timbuktu sing about Moussa ag Litni. Do you want to hear it?'

'Go on then,' said Sophie.

'It won't give you nightmares?'

'Of course not,' said Sophie.

Gidaado started to drum out a rhythm on Sophie's shoulders. *Dum baba-dum baba-dum baba-dum*. He took a deep breath and began to sing.

> *'Relax and open up your ears*
> *And listen to my story,*
> *But I should warn you straight away*
> *That it is rather gory.*
>
> *Moussa ag Litni*
> *Fills all our hearts with dread.*
> *He loves to steal camels*
> *And leave their owners dead.*

He wears a big blue turban
'Cos he doesn't like the sun,
And round his neck he wears a bell
So if you hear it – run!'

'Sorry to interrupt,' said Sophie, 'but that doesn't make sense. This man is a camel thief, right? So what's he doing wearing a bell? Why does he want people to know he's coming?'

'Moussa ag Litni likes killing people and stealing their camels, but he likes it even more if he gets to chase them first. He wears the bell to give his victims a chance to run away.'

'That's sick,' said Sophie.

'Can I carry on?' said Gidaado.

'Only if you stop using my head and shoulders as drums.'

'Okay, I'll use Chobbal's bottom.'

Dum baba-dum baba-dum baba-dum...

'Alai was a little boy
Alai was only eight,
He had a buck-toothed camel,
They were the best of mates.'

'Look,' said Sophie, craning her neck round to face Gidaado, 'if this lad Alai ends up getting killed by Moussa ag Litni, you can save your breath. I don't want to hear it.'

'Suit yourself,' said Gidaado.

They rode on a while in silence. The sun was low and the children and the camel cast long, eerie shadows on the drifting sand. Sophie tried to forget the song but she couldn't. What had happened to little Alai?

'All right,' she said at last. 'Finish the song.'

'Sure?'

'Yes.'

'Okay, here goes.'

Dum baba-dum baba-dum baba-dum . . .

> *'One day the buck-toothed camel*
> *Was drinking at a well.*
> *Alai was fast asleep nearby*
> *And didn't hear the bell.*
>
> *Ag Litni stood before him,*
> *Pulled out a silver knife,*
> *He said, "I've come to take away*
> *Your camel and your life."*

"Don't hurt me," Alai snivelled,
And he grovelled on his knees.
"You're welcome to the camel –
Just leave me in one piece."

"All right, I'll show you mercy,
I'd hate to kill a tot."
Ag Litni smiled crookedly
And then he whispered, "Not!"

Ag Litni he began to dance,
His knife whirled round his head,
Ag Litni he got dizzy
And poor Alai got dead.

So if YOU have a camel
You'll have to be on guard,
'Cos ag Litni knows where you live
And he's extremely hard.'

Sophie shuddered and glanced around her
fearfully. On every side the level sands
stretched away to a flat horizon. She listened.

23

There was no sound except the tread of Chobbal's hooves in the soft sand.

'Why don't the police arrest ag Litni?' asked Sophie.

'No one knows where he lives. He could be anywhere in the Sahara Desert. They say he moves around a lot. One time, three policemen from Gorom-Gorom were sent out into the desert on camels to look for ag Litni. They had guns and radios and everything.'

'And?'

'Never seen again,' said Gidaado.

Dusk loomed around them. Sophie looked over at the sun and it was now the colour of blood.

'What about you?' said Sophie. 'You still travel through the desert with Chobbal like this.'

'My grandmother is sick. I have to go to Gorom-Gorom every week to buy her medicine.'

'But don't you ever get frightened?'

Gidaado laughed uneasily and glanced around him. 'Sometimes,' he said.

24

Sophie didn't want to ask the next question. 'Are you frightened *now*?' she said.

'My knees would be knocking if there wasn't a camel between them,' said Gidaado. 'It's not quite so bad when I have someone with me, though.'

Sophie frowned. So *that* was why he had invited her to come for a ride. It wasn't that he wanted to be friends. He just didn't want to be alone when ag Litni showed up.

'To tell the truth,' continued Gidaado, 'Moussa ag Litni is not the biggest danger out here in the desert.'

'What is the biggest danger?' said Sophie.

'Djinns,' said Gidaado. 'Desert djinns. People are always telling stories about them. They creep up behind you and then they jump on your head and make you go mad. But only if you are on your own, of course.'

'Right,' said Sophie. 'And is there anything else I should know about?'

'No, I don't think so.'

'I can't believe you didn't let me know all this before we set out,' said Sophie.

'If I had, you wouldn't have come with me,' said Gidaado.

'You're dead right I wouldn't,' said Sophie.

Chapter 4

Sophie found it hard to stay mad at Gidaado for long. She felt sorry for him more than anything. He had to do this journey every week, with nothing to take his mind off Moussa ag Litni and the desert djinns. Besides, she thought, the Sahara was a very big place indeed. The chances of running into Moussa ag Litni here were nineteen gazillion to one. And if she and Gidaado stayed together, they would not be attacked by desert djinns either.

On the horizon, Sophie saw the outline of a tree. It was a very odd-looking tree with a big, thick trunk and ugly, stubby branches. Dad had pointed out one of these to her before, but she had forgotten its name.

'Baobab,' said Gidaado, as if reading her mind. 'When God created the baobab tree, she was the most beautiful of all the trees, with long, graceful branches and fine leaves. But she got proud and began to boast about her beauty, so God took her out of the ground and stuck her back in upside down. What you see there are actually the roots.'

Sophie laughed. She would have to tell Dad that story when she got back home. Thinking of home, she felt a sudden pang of guilt; there was now no way that she was going to be back home by bedtime. Her dad would certainly be worried, and he might even call the police. She imagined him at the police station trying to explain in Fulfulde that his daughter was missing. Dad's Fulfulde was not as good as hers and he was bound to get all confused and upset.

'How much further to your village, Gidaado?' said Sophie.

'Not far now. We'll stop at the baobab tree for something to eat and drink.'

'But you just ate the last banana.'

'God will provide,' said Gidaado.

Before long, Chobbal arrived at the baobab tree. '*Bahaat-ugh!*' said Gidaado and the camel stopped.

Gidaado reached up and took hold of an over-hanging branch, then lifted his legs off the camel and hung there in midair.

'Come on, Sofa,' he said. 'Let's go.'

'Where?' said Sophie. 'Let's go where?'

'Follow me,' said Gidaado, making his way along the branch hand over hand.

Sophie reached up and grabbed the branch above her head. Slowly she let it take her weight and then she started to follow Gidaado, who had nearly reached the trunk now. Sophie looked down at her feet dangling uselessly beneath her. She was just about high enough off the ground to be scared.

When Sophie looked up again, Gidaado was nowhere to be seen.

'Gidaado!' she called.

Silence.

'Gidaado the Fourth, where are you?' Sophie shouted.

'In here,' came a muffled voice – it seemed to be coming from *inside* the tree. 'I'm looking for some matches,' said the voice.

Sophie swung her way along to the heart of the tree, where the trunk split off into three fat branches. She looked down into a gaping black hole. The trunk was completely hollow.

'Just drop down!' came Gidaado's voice out of the darkness. 'It's not far.'

'No way,' shouted Sophie. 'I can't see the bottom.'

'Suit yourself,' called Gidaado, 'but there is a nest of fire ants on the end of that branch, just where your hands are now.'

Sophie dropped.

'OUCH,' she said. 'You said it wasn't far.'

'I also said there was a nest of fire ants up there,' said Gidaado. 'I lie sometimes.'

'Remind me never to believe anything you say ever again,' said Sophie.

'Okay,' said Gidaado.

The light of a match flared, and Sophie saw Gidaado's white teeth grinning at her. Then the light grew brighter – some kind of paraffin lamp had been lit.

The lamp cast an orange glow on the smooth wooden walls of the little chamber. There were shelves on the walls, stacked with strange things. On one shelf there was a row of calabash bowls of different sizes and then something that looked like a banjo with three strings. On another shelf there was an assortment of fruit – it was mostly baobab fruit, but there were also guavas and a bag of dates. On another there was a bicycle chain, a catapult and an enormous straw hat.

'We'll stop here for a while and have something to eat,' said Gidaado, 'and then carry on. My village is less than an hour's ride from here, and Chobbal knows the way even in the dark. My grandmother will give you a straw mat to sleep on and in the morning my uncle Ibrahiim can take you home on his motorbike.'

Sophie thought of home and swallowed hard. If only there was some way she could let Dad know she was safe and that she would be home in the morning. If I were president of this country, she thought, I would put some telephone boxes in the Sahara. Or even better, a mobile phone mast. Then children could explore the desert freely without their dads worrying about them.

Sophie sat down on a small wooden stool. She had to admit that this was a great den. No one looking at the baobab tree from the outside would imagine there was such a comfortable little room inside.

'Griots used to be buried in baobab trees when they died,' said Gidaado. 'People thought that griots had strange supernatural powers and that the crops wouldn't grow properly if there was a griot in the ground. So when a griot died they would just wrap his body in a sheet and stick it in a baobab tree. All my ancestors were put in baobab trees, right up to Gidaado the Third.'

Sophie nodded. Why did people have to be like that? Just because the griots were a bit different from everyone else, people were frightened of them and treated them as odd. Sophie knew what that felt like, and she hated it.

Gidaado emptied the dates into a calabash bowl. 'That should be enough for the three of us,' he said.

'*Three?*' said Sophie.

'Oh yes, I forgot. That is Tijani.'

Sophie looked where Gidaado's finger was pointing, but she did not see anything. Then she noticed a big mottled lizard high up on the wall. It blended in perfectly with the wood of the tree trunk. The lizard looked at Sophie and blinked, and she could have sworn it smiled at her.

Gidaado clicked deep down in his throat, and the lizard darted down the wall and over to where the boy was sitting. It took a date in its mouth and scurried back up the wall again.

'He's a skink,' said Gidaado. 'I call him Tijani because he has two fingers missing on one of his hands, like my great-great-grandfather.'

'And what's that?' asked Sophie, pointing at the strange banjo.

'That's my *hoddu*. All griots play the *hoddu*, it's part of the job.'

'Can you play something for me now?'

'Okay.'

Gidaado took the *hoddu*, perched it on his knee, and began to pluck the strings with his thumb and two fingers. The music was mellow and mystical. Gidaado swelled and began to sing softly:

'Click of a gecko,
Sigh of a camel,
Skitter of skinks on a rock.
Spurgle of thick, sweet tea
poured into a glass from up high,
Croaking of oasis frogs.

The desert rejoices and I with it.
Praise to the Creator.

Donkeys gazing at the evening star,
Ants in a monkey-nut shell,
Vultures waiting on the cypress tree at dawn,
Goat kids gambolling by the well.

34

The desert rejoices and I with it.
Praise to the Creator.

Chickens dancing in the dust,
A girl dancing as she pounds millet,
The flame of our lamp dancing
as it drinks its last drops of paraffin.

The desert dances and I with it.
Praise to the—'

Gidaado froze, and his eyes widened.

Sophie frowned. 'Why have you—'

'*Shhh.*'

Sophie listened hard. At first she heard nothing, and then a faint sound. The sound was very quiet but getting louder all the time. It was the tinkling of a bell.

Sophie glanced at Gidaado and saw that his legs were shaking. *This could not be happening.*

The tinkling stopped, and a high-pitched voice spoke.

'Funny-looking thing, isn't he, Chief?' said the voice. It was coming from just outside the tree.

35

'He's an albino,' said a different voice, low and menacing. 'He will fetch a good price at Tasmakat market. Or perhaps he will make a good chaser.'

Gidaado was trembling all over now. *It's him*, he mouthed. *It's Moussa ag Litni.*

'Oooh, Chief,' said the high-pitched voice, 'look at these big strong teeth.'

Gidaado was shaking so much that the calabash fell off his lap and onto the floor. Dates went everywhere.

Sophie bit her lip.

'What was that?' said Moussa ag Litni.

'I said, "Oooh, look at these big strong teeth."'

'No, what was that noise?'

'What noise?'

'There is someone inside the tree,' said ag Litni.

Chapter 5

'*Salam alaykum!*' called ag Litni cheerily. 'Who's there?'

Gidaado opened his mouth and then shut it again, much to Sophie's relief. It was rude not to return the greeting, but rude was better than dead.

'Go on then, Usman, you halfwit,' said ag Litni. 'Climb up and tell me who's in there.'

'Okay, Chief,' said the voice.

There was a scrabbling sound on the trunk of

the tree. Gidaado leaned over Sophie and blew the paraffin lamp out, plunging them into darkness.

Sophie's eyes were fixed on the circle of faint light at the opening to the trunk above them. Her heart seemed to be pounding out the rhythm of Little Alai inside her chest. *DUM BABA-DUM BABA-DUM BABA-DUM.* The scrabbling stopped and a face appeared above – a wrinkled, leathery face swathed in a black turban. She could just make out a pair of black eyes staring down into the tree.

'Ah yes,' said the voice. 'There he is. Shall I kill him?'

Sophie felt the pit of her stomach suddenly go ice cold. Gidaado had been seen, and now she would be seen, too.

'Of course not,' said ag Litni. 'I shall kill him myself. You can pull him out but I'll do the Death Dance. Is it a man or a child?'

This can not be happening. This can not be happening.

'Neither,' said the voice above them. 'It's a skink.'

38

'Oh.' The voice sounded disappointed. 'A skink?'

'Yes, a skink.'

'That's no fun. You can have him.'

Tijani! Tijani was up above them still, near the opening of the trunk. Why had he stayed up there and let himself be spotted?

A hand reached down and took hold of Tijani round the middle. The lizard was lifted up out of the tree, and then the hand and the face were gone. There was some scrabbling and the soft thud of someone landing on the ground outside.

'Let's go,' said ag Litni. 'You ride Nyiiri, I'll ride the albino.'

'Aren't we going to do what we did on Tuesday, Chief? Bury ourselves in the sand and lie quietly until the owner of the camel comes back, and then leap out and do the Dance? That was fun.'

'If you like,' said ag Litni. 'Or better still, you could bury yourself in the sand and stay there.'

A camel grunted. The bell tinkled again, but it seemed further away now.

'*Zorki!* Chief, that boss-eyed skink just *bit* me.'

'Never mind. Think of tonight's skink soup.'

39

The voices died away and there was a long, uncomfortable silence.

'Have they gone?' whispered Gidaado at last.

'I think so,' whispered Sophie.

A match flared and Gidaado lit the lamp again. 'I can't believe Moussa ag Litni just stole Chobbal and Tijani,' he said. 'If I ever see him, I'll give him a piece of my mind.'

'And various other pieces of yourself, too, when he starts his Death Dance on you,' said Sophie. 'You should be glad you're alive.'

'I am. I thought we were goners. The griots of Timbuktu would have written songs about our horrible death inside the baobab tree.'

'Do you mind if we get out of this hole?' said Sophie. 'It's giving me the creeps.'

'Okay. Pass me that rope just behind you.'

Sophie screamed and spun round.

'What's wrong?' said Gidaado, alarmed.

'Oh, I see,' said Sophie, 'you mean *rope* rope. Sorry.'

Gidaado put four guavas and a baobab fruit in Sophie's shoulder bag. Then he took the coil of rope, made a noose in one end and threw it upwards. It caught on the stump of a branch just by the entrance to the hole. He tugged hard on it and then stood back to let Sophie climb up.

'Good throw,' said Sophie, taking hold of the rope. She climbed up and out into the branches of the baobab tree. The air was cool and fresh after what felt like a long imprisonment.

Gidaado appeared beside her and pointed at a thin branch to her right. 'That's the easiest way down,' he said. 'I'll show you.'

He swung down onto the thin branch and made his way along it hand over hand. As he went along, the branch bent, lowering him gently towards the ground. Finally he let go and dropped down onto the sand below. The branch sprang back up with a funny *boing* sound.

Sophie got down the same way and looked around her. There was a faint glow in the west where the sun had set, but the rest of the sky was dark grey. One or two bright stars were already appearing.

Gidaado was a little distance away, scanning the ground. 'Here are the tracks,' he said. 'Come on.'

'Wait, what do you mean? What tracks?'

'Chobbal,' said Gidaado. 'He went this way.'

'You're not serious,' said Sophie. 'You intend to go after Chobbal?'

'Of course. I want him back.'

'Listen to yourself,' said Sophie, suddenly getting frightened again. 'You were as scared as I was in there. You said yourself we're lucky to be alive. And now you want to *follow Moussa ag Litni*.'

'If we don't follow him now, the wind will cover over these tracks and we'll have lost Chobbal for ever.'

Sophie could not believe she was hearing this. 'Gidaado, he's a camel. Yes he's white, yes he's special, but he's a camel. He is not worth risking our lives for.'

Gidaado folded his arms and looked down. Then he looked up at the sky. 'Sofa, you see that star up there in the east, about three fists above the horizon.'

Sophie looked. 'What about it?'

'We call that star Puchu. Walk straight towards it and after about an hour you will see the light of

42

a fire in front of you. That's Giriiji, my village. You will see four round huts and a square one. Go to the square hut, knock on the door and a wrinkly old woman with great long earlobes will open it. She will shout at you and call you names and say, "Why have you woken me up? I'm a very sick woman." That's my grandmother. Tell her I sent you, and she will look after you well. And in the morning my Uncle Ibrahiim will take you back to Gorom-Gorom on his motorbike.'

Sophie stared. 'What about you?'

'I told you. I have a friend to rescue.'

Sophie looked at Gidaado as he stood there shivering in his too-long sleeves and baggy trousers. As she looked at him she noticed something for the first time. Underneath Gidaado's fear there was a deep well of courage. It was the same kind of courage Tijani had when he let himself be taken out of the tree trunk. The kind of courage that enables you to put yourself in danger for the sake of a friend.

'I'll come with you,' Sophie heard herself saying.

Chapter 6

'How long do you think we have been walking?' said Sophie.

'Two hours, maybe three,' said Gidaado.

The children were following the camel tracks northwards through the dark desert. The tracks were plain to see, each one a neat oval split down the middle. There were two sets of tracks, one belonging to Moussa ag Litni's camel, the other to Chobbal. When the sun had gone down, it had got very dark indeed – they had needed to bend right over to see where the tracks were. But now the moon was coming up – a clear three-quarter moon which cast a very faint, ghostly light over the entire landscape.

Sophie glanced over at Gidaado. His eyes were big and worried.

'You really love Chobbal, don't you?' said Sophie.

'Nothing much to love,' said Gidaado. 'He's a bit stupid, he eats too much and he is always wandering off and getting lost. I have to spend half my time out looking for him.'

'But you do love him.'

'I feel responsible for him,' said Gidaado. 'You can't give a camel his milk every day for two years and not feel responsible for him, can you?'

'You called him a friend.'

'We get on together, all right? He doesn't spit or kick, unlike some camels I know. And he sometimes smiles when he sees me.'

'That's sweet.'

'Doesn't stop him trotting off happily with murderous Tuareg bandits, though, does it?'

'He doesn't know how wicked they are,' said Sophie.

Gidaado clicked his tongue. 'He will soon.'

'What do you mean?'

'Let's just say that Moussa ag Litni does not treat his camels very kindly.'

Sophie looked down at Chobbal's hoofprints in the sand and she scowled. Sophie hated cruelty to animals, however big or small they were. Just last Thursday she had got up at midnight, crept into her dad's study and set free a whole box of soldier ants which he had been planning to feed to his desert flytrap. Dad never realised it was her; the next morning he had wandered around for a whole hour, murmuring, 'Where on earth did I put those ants?'

Sophie wanted to ask Gidaado about the camels, but she was not sure she wanted to hear the answers. Eventually curiosity got the better of her.

'What does he do to them?' she asked.

'What does who do to who?'

'What does Moussa ag Litni do to the camels?'

Gidaado sighed. 'They say that when ag Litni steals a camel he tries it out for a while to see what its strengths and weaknesses are. Then he puts it in one of three categories. If the camel is fast, it becomes a chaser. If the camel is strong, it becomes a puller. If the camel is neither fast nor strong, it gets taken to Mali and sold at one of the camel markets there.'

'What does he use the chasers for?'

'To chase people and steal more camels, of course. Ag Litni must have been riding a chaser tonight, when he spotted Chobbal.'

'What do the pullers do?'

'They draw water. Haven't you seen the wells in the Sahara desert?'

'Not really,' said Sophie. 'I've never been this far north.'

'The water is so far under the ground that the wells have to be super-deep – at least fifty metres. That's about three baobab trees. You try drawing water from a fifty-metre well. You have to lift fifty metres of rope plus a big bucket of water.'

'I see what you mean,' said Sophie. 'You must need big muscles.'

'Not enough,' said Gidaado. 'You need a camel. A donkey could do it but a camel is better. You tie one end of the rope to your camel and the other end to a bucket, and you ride the camel to and fro to draw water.'

'What's wrong with that?' said Sophie. 'That's not cruel, is it?'

'It is when Moussa ag Litni is in charge. He wants to have the strongest camels in the Sahara so he makes his pullers draw water all day with hardly any rest. The rope cuts into the camels' shoulders and they get so tired they often collapse.'

'That's horrible,' said Sophie.

'Life as a chaser isn't much better,' said Gidaado. 'They say that ag Litni isn't content for a camel just to be fast – it has to be fast over long distances. So he takes it on long training runs through the desert, running for hours and hours. If it slows down, he beats it; if it falls over, he beats it. Without pain there is never a gain, he says.'

'We have a proverb like that too,' said Sophie.

'That's why ag Litni loves camel chases. He knows that his camels have enough stamina to keep going for as long as it takes. Sooner or later his victim's camel will get tired and stop. Ag Litni always wins.'

Sophie thought of Chobbal. If ag Litni found out how fast Chobbal could run, he was sure to make him a chaser. She looked over at Gidaado, who blinked a few times and wiped his eyes.

'You're crying,' said Sophie.

'I'm not. There's a bit of sand in my eye.'

'Have a guava,' said Sophie.

In the darkness ahead of her, Sophie thought she saw the shape of a hut. She grabbed Gidaado's arm and whispered, 'Is that it? Is that where Moussa ag Litni lives?'

Gidaado stared long and hard and then he shook his head. 'No,' he said. 'I think Uncle Ibrahiim has talked about this place. It belongs to a nomadic family from Mali. They only stay here for about three days in every year.'

As the children got closer, it became clear that Gidaado's guess was right. The camel tracks did not go to the hut, but led past it and away into the distance. The hut itself was a low dome made out of millet stalk mats, with a very low doorway – *like a straw igloo*, thought Sophie. The hut did not seem to be occupied; it was in a very bad state of repair, with large holes in its mat walls. It looked as if goats had been eating it.

'No one there,' said Gidaado. 'There's probably nothing inside but a water-pot.'

Water. Just what we need, thought Sophie, whose bottle was nearly empty. She ran to the hut and ducked in through the doorway. It was very dark inside, but chinks of moonlight came in through the holes in the mat walls. It was completely bare except for a wooden bed and a large clay water-pot. Sophie lifted the lid.

Empty.

Sophie heard Gidaado laughing outside the hut.

'I said a water-pot, Sofa. I did not say there would be water in it.'

Sophie tutted in annoyance and turned to leave and it was then that she heard the low hissing sound. She froze and looked where the sound was coming from. And there it was, coiled around the frame of the doorway, its terrible unblinking glare fixed upon her. Sophie was staring into the eyes of a spitting cobra, one of the most poisonous snakes in the world.

Chapter 7

'*Gidaado*,' squeaked Sophie. 'Gidaado, come here.'

Gidaado appeared at the doorway of the hut. He opened his mouth to speak but then saw the look of horror on Sophie's face.

'*Rope*,' Sophie whispered. 'A spitting rope, right there.'

Gidaado looked where she was pointing. Ever so slowly he unbuttoned his shirt, took it

52

off and stepped up beside the snake. He was within a couple of metres of it.

'OI! LEGLESS!' he shouted, waving the bright yellow shirt. 'Here's what the best-dressed ropes of the Sahara are wearing this season!' The cobra twisted angrily towards Gidaado, glared into his eyes and reared up to spit.

Gidaado threw the shirt. It fell neatly over the snake's head and immediately an enraged hissing came from inside it.

'Run!' shouted Gidaado.

Sophie ran past the writhing yellow shirt, past Gidaado, out of the hut and away into the desert, and only when she could run no further did she stop and look back. Gidaado was not far behind her.

'What about your shirt?' asked Sophie, as he came up alongside her, panting.

'I decided it was safer to let the rope keep it. Besides, I think yellow suited the rope better than it suited me.'

In running away, the children had strayed far away from the camel tracks, so now they turned and walked west, scanning the ground carefully as they went.

'You did not even seem scared back there,' said Sophie.

'I wasn't. I didn't think *you* were scared of ropes, either,' said Gidaado.

'What gave you that idea?'

'I saw you at Salif dan Bari's stall at the market. You were within three metres of Mamadou the Malevolent Mamba and you didn't look scared at all.'

'Mamadou has no fangs,' said Sophie. 'I thought everyone knew that.'

'Really?' Gidaado looked amazed. 'Are you sure?'

'That's what comes of living in a village in the middle of nowhere,' said Sophie. 'You miss out on the town gossip.'

'You mean Salif dan Bari is a fraud?'

'Yes. But a nice fraud. A funny fraud.' Sophie looked at Gidaado. 'You didn't buy...?'

'I did, as it happens.' Gidaado put his hand in his trouser pocket and fished out three small blue pills. 'Are you telling me that Salif snake

54

pills don't work?'

'They're just sugar mixed with blue berries,' said Sophie, laughing.

'So if that rope in the hut back there had bitten me—'

'You would soon be dead.'

Gidaado put his hand to his mouth. '*Zorki*, Sofa,' he said. 'If I'd have known that, I would never have called him Legless or attacked him with my shirt.'

'Oh really?' said Sophie.

'No, I'd have run away as fast as a rabbit.'

'And left me stranded in the hut with a spitting rope?'

'Yes. No. Er—'

Sophie laughed at his embarrassment. 'I'm glad you rescued me, Gidaado. Thank you.'

Gidaado stopped suddenly and Sophie almost bumped into him. 'There!' he said, pointing over to the left. 'Those are Chobbal's tracks.'

Sophie took her water bottle out of her bag and they each had a sip before setting off again, following the tracks northwards.

'So you saw me at the rope man's stall?' said Sophie.

'I see you most market days,' said Gidaado. 'You do stand out in a crowd. Everyone always knows what the white girl is doing.'

'But you never said anything to me.'

'I didn't know what to say,' said Gidaado.

'Hello would have been a good start,' said Sophie crossly.

'Don't be like that,' said Gidaado. 'We're friends now, aren't we?'

'Are we?'

'We must be. I saved your life.'

'Only by accident.'

'Well, let's have a guava to celebrate.'

'All right.' Sophie took the last two guavas out of her bag and gave one to Gidaado.

'Here's a riddle for you,' said Gidaado, biting into his guava. 'Are you ready?'

'Go on.'

'I have three sons. One goes away but never comes back, one eats but is never full, one lies down but never gets up. Who am I and who are my sons?'

'Eats but is never full,' said Sophie. 'That sounds like someone I know.'

'Very funny,' said Gidaado, spitting out a mouthful of guava seeds.

'Falls down but never gets up. Is it someone who has died?'

'No.'

'But it *is* a person?'

'No.'

'Animal?'

'No.'

'What then?'

'I'm not telling,' said Gidaado. 'Work it out.'

They walked on in silence. Sophie was thinking hard about the riddle, to take her mind off Chobbal and Tijani. The moon shone on the still sands and the silence all around was so profound that Sophie's ears began to ring. She was grateful when Gidaado spoke again.

'Hey, Sofa!'

'What?'

'Do you have any water left?'

'A tiny bit. We should probably save it till later.'

As long as there was water in her bottle, Sophie knew they had a chance. But once it was all gone, they would be in a very dangerous situation. *Never mess with the Sahara Desert,* her dad used to say. If only she had listened to him.

'Gidaado, when you travel in the desert, what's the longest you've ever gone without drinking?'

'Three or four hours,' said Gidaado. 'But I could go longer if I had to. My great-great-great-great-great-great-great-great-grandfather, Hussein the Tall, once went three whole days without drinking water, just to win a bet.'

Sophie looked at her watch but even in the moonlight she could not make out the time. She frowned. How much longer before they would come to ag Litni's settlement?

'If you die in the desert,' said Gidaado brightly, 'do you know what happens to you?'

'Yes, you rot. You become a skeleton and the sun whitens your bones.

'That's what most people think,' said Gidaado, 'but it is not true. You do not rot.'

'So what happens?'

'The heat of the desert sucks all of the liquid out of you and your skin becomes like brittle leather. You shrivel a bit but you don't rot.'

'Thank you for telling me,' said Sophie.

'You're welcome,' said Gidaado. 'Do you want to hear a song about it?'

'No,' said Sophie firmly.

'Do you want to hear another song about ag Litni?'

'No.'

'Do you want me to sing you some more of my *tarik*?'

'No.'

'There's no pleasing some people,' said Gidaado the Fourth. 'In that case, I'll just have to – aaaaargh!'

'Gidaado!' screamed Sophie, and grabbed his arm. The sand beneath his feet had given way and he was falling through it.

Chapter 8

Only Gidaado's head and one arm were visible above the sand. Sophie hung on to the arm and pulled for all she was worth. Gidaado's shoulders appeared, then his other arm. Sophie pulled him all the way out of the hole and lay back on the sand, exhausted.

'What just happened?' said Sophie.

'That used to be a well,' said Gidaado breathlessly. 'Many years ago it must have belonged to the settlement we passed. When a well is abandoned, it gradually fills up with sand and dust until you can't tell that there is a hole there at all.'

'Until you step on it,' said Sophie.

'Right. It is just loose sand, after all. If anything heavier than a skink steps in the wrong place, it will fall right through and the sand will close over it. It's incredibly dangerous.'

'Someone should put a big sign next to it,' said Sophie.

Gidaado was still in shock. His eyes were wider than usual and his voice was shaking. 'If you hadn't grabbed my arm like that,' he said, 'I would not be here now.'

'You mean I saved your life? So we're equal now.'

'Maybe.' Gidaado leaned over and felt his ankle. 'I think I twisted it,' he said, wincing in pain.

'Can you walk?'

Gidaado got up, hobbled a few agonising paces and sat down again.

'No. It's bad.'

Sophie felt sick. She had completely relied on Gidaado so far. If he couldn't walk, how would they ever rescue Chobbal? And they could not turn back, either. Panic rose in her stomach.

'So what do we do now?' she said. 'We just stay here and wait for help to arrive, do we? This isn't exactly Clapham Junction, is it? It might be six months before anyone comes past. And if anyone does come, it'll probably be Moussa ag Litni or one of his psychopathic friends. But that won't matter, because we will be dead of thirst by that time. The heat will make us shrivel up and turn into leather people, and by Thursday we won't be of any use to anybody, except perhaps a Tuareg cushion-maker.' Sophie choked on these last words and burst into tears.

Gidaado gazed up at her with interest. 'What's Clapham Junction?' he said.

She turned on him furiously. 'Yes, that's right, let's have a nice little talk about Clapham Junction. We have plenty of time, after all. I'll tell you about Clapham Junction, and you tell me about your village, and I'll tell you about carnivorous plants, and you tell me about skinks, and so on and so on, and then by the time we die of thirst, at least we'll be *CLEVER LEATHER PEOPLE*!'

62

It felt good to shout at someone. Gidaado was staring at her with his mouth open – maybe he thought that a desert djinn had jumped on her head and sent her mad. Or perhaps he was simply not used to being yelled at by a girl. Sophie went and sat down next to him on the sand. She felt very small and scared.

'What are we going to do?' she said.

'You drink the rest of the water,' said Gidaado quietly. 'Then follow the tracks to Moussa ag Litni's settlement and rescue Chobbal. Bring him back here and we'll go home.'

Sophie did not reply at once. The last thing she wanted was to continue on her own, but deep down she knew he was right. They needed a camel to carry Gidaado, and there was only one way of getting one.

'All right, I'll go,' said Sophie, and wondered at how small her voice sounded in this vast, dark desert. She opened her bag and gave Gidaado the baobab fruit, to keep him happy while he waited. She tried to give him the water bottle too, but Gidaado refused to take it.

'You need that more than I do,' he said.

'How far away do you think ag Litni's settlement is?' asked Sophie.

'Not too far. The man who took Tijani said they would have him in their soup tonight. I think they were expecting to arrive home before midnight.'

'If I'm following on foot it will take me longer, won't it?'

'Yes,' said Gidaado, 'but that's a good thing. When you arrive, everyone will already be asleep.'

'We hope,' said Sophie.

'Find Chobbal, get on his back, and get out of there as fast as you can.'

'Right,' said Sophie.

'And pray that Moussa ag Litni doesn't wake up.'

'Right.'

Sophie walked away, following the tracks. It was not particularly cold, but she noticed that her hands were trembling.

'Sophie!' shouted Gidaado. She stopped and turned round.

'What now?'

'Be careful.'

64

Sophie turned and walked on. That was something, at least. She was no longer Sofa but Sophie. Perhaps at last she had a friend in Africa.

Walking alone in the desert was not Sophie's idea of a good night out. She kept telling herself there was nothing to be afraid of, but it did not help. She knew there was quite a lot to be afraid of, not least the desert djinns that Gidaado had told her about. *They creep up behind you and jump on your head and make you go mad.* Sophie turned around and listened. Nothing there but sand and rocks. She walked on.

The landscape was dotted with strange twisted shapes, which waved their hideous thorny arms at Sophie as she passed. *They are only acacia bushes*, she told herself. Plants are nothing to be frightened of, unless you happen to be an ant and the plant happens to be carnivorous. Sophie began to wonder if there existed carnivorous plants bigger than the flytraps her dad studied. Plants big enough to eat a frog, perhaps. Or a goat. Or a child. She drank the last of the water in her bottle and walked on, trembling.

Sophie walked with her head down, concentrating on the camel tracks in front of her. She had walked for almost an hour when suddenly she realised that it was getting darker; a thick cloud had passed in front of the moon and cut off the light. The wind was getting up – at first it was just a breeze, then stronger and stronger gusts. Sophie put her hand up to her face and walked faster. Great drifts of sand were blowing across her path. She started to run.

The air was now thick with sand. It was so dark that Sophie could no longer see the ground, not even her hand in front of her face. This was a real sandstorm, like the one that little Fatimata Tamboura had got lost in only last year. *Never mess with the Sahara Desert.*

Dad had told her many times what to do in a sandstorm. *Sit down right where you are*, he always said, *and wait for it to pass*. Sophie sat down, put her head in her hands and waited. Sharp grains of sand bombarded her, stinging her ears and the back of her neck and hands. Sophie supposed that she was now an easy target for any djinns who happened to be passing. She sat totally still, bracing herself against the wind and counting the minutes as they passed. She fully expected something evil to jump on her head any moment.

But the desert djinns did not come. *Perhaps*, thought Sophie, *they are all sitting with their heads in their hands wishing the storm would pass. Or perhaps they don't exist.*

After ten minutes the wind began to calm down and after twenty minutes the air was still. Sophie took her hands away from her face and brushed sand out of her hair and her ears.

The moon was out again but everything looked different now. The sand on the ground was deeper than before. All trace of the camel tracks was gone.

Go back, was Sophie's first thought. *Go back to Gidaado and explain what has happened.* But how would she ever find him? And what would they do then? They would be in a worse situation than before, with no camel to ride, no water to drink and no tracks to follow. The only way was forward. Sophie stood up and set off in the direction she had been walking when the storm hit. *Please don't let it be far,* she thought.

On and on Sophie walked, and with each step she felt hope ebbing away. Then she saw a huge sand dune looming out of the darkness. Not wanting to veer off to the left or right, she decided to go straight over the top.

Normally Sophie would have run up the sand dune. She loved the feeling of the heavy sand sliding away beneath her feet. Running up a sand dune was a bit like running up a 'DOWN' escalator, except you didn't get shouted at for it. But Sophie did not run up this dune. In fact, she could hardly get up it at all. It was early morning and tiredness was overcoming her. Since leaving the baobab tree she had hardly stopped walking, and that was many hours ago. Up and up Sophie plodded, and with each step she wanted nothing more than to lie down in the soft sand and go to sleep.

But what Sophie saw when she got to the top of the dune made all her tiredness disappear in a moment.

Chapter 9

Spread out below Sophie was a flat plain surrounded by dunes. In the middle of the plain a campfire was burning dimly, and around the fire were four large canvas tents. There was also a fenced pen full of camels. A strange mixture of relief and fear flooded over her and made her feel giddy. This was Moussa ag Litni's camp.

Sophie lay down on her stomach and looked at the tents. They were dark and their entrances were tightly closed up. If anyone had been outside by the fire, the sandstorm would have driven them in. There was no sound coming from the tents. *They're all asleep*, Sophie told herself, willing herself to believe it.

Next she turned her attention to the camels. There were about twenty of them crammed into the small pen, all kneeling down. Sophie craned her neck, on the lookout for a pale hump amongst the dark ones. And there he was! *Chobbal!* He was on the edge of the group with his head raised, sniffing the air.

In the shadow of the furthest dune, Sophie noticed a small circular wall with a bar across it, which could only be one thing. A well! She was so thirsty, she was tempted to go and have a drink straight away, but then she remembered what Gidaado had said. To draw water in the desert you need more than big muscles. *You need a camel.*

Sophie knew that she would have to go down to the pen. She almost wished that the storm would come back to give her some cover. But now the air was still and the moon was high in the sky, casting an eerie light over the tents and the camels. Sophie stood up, took a few deep breaths and began to run down the sand dune towards the pen.

Before coming to Africa, Sophie had a recurring nightmare which always ended up with her being chased by a gigantic spider. In the dream, she would try to run fast but her feet would move horribly slowly. That was exactly how Sophie felt running down the dune. With each step her feet sank in the sand. It was like running in slow motion. She glanced across at the tents as she flailed down the slope. *Don't come out, ag Litni. Please don't come out.*

Sophie ran behind the enclosure, flung herself to the ground and listened. Still no sound from the tents. The fence was a big circle of thorn branches laid on top of each other, which was the traditional way of enclosing animals or crops. Sophie started to pull branches out of the way to make a hole wide enough for a camel's legs. Vicious thorns pricked her fingers and arms but she did not care. All she could think was, *Get in quickly, get out quickly.*

71

As soon as the gap was big enough, Sophie crawled into the pen and in amongst the camels. Some of them gazed at her with lazy interest but most just carried on sleeping. She crawled over to Chobbal and stroked his snowy neck. The albino cocked his head on one side and gave her a wide buck-toothed smile. Sophie saw with relief that he was still wearing his saddle. Everything was going perfectly.

Then the door of one of the tents opened and there was the sound of footsteps hurrying towards the pen.

Chapter 10

The footsteps stopped just the other side of the fence from where Sophie was crouching. Through the thorn branches she could make out the shape of a man, wrapped in a blanket and bending over. There was a loud retch and then the foul spattering sound of vomit on sand.

The stench of sick wafted into the pen, and one or two of the camels looked up and snorted in disgust. Sophie pressed herself closer to the ground.

There were more footsteps and then a woman's voice:

'Where are you, Usman?'

A loud groan gave her the answer.

'Usman, I *told* you not to eat any of that soup,' said the woman. 'I *told* you Aisseta wouldn't cook it right. That young girl doesn't know one end of a skink from the other. She probably didn't even take the bile glands out.'

More retching, and the revolting splatter of regurgitated skink soup.

The woman came into view between the gaps in the fence. She was wearing a long black shawl and silver coins glinted in her hair. Sophie could not see the woman's face, but she did not sound happy.

'Did you not realise you were the only one actually eating the stuff? For goodness' sake, Usman, even Aisseta herself didn't have any.'

'I feel a fever coming on. I'm going to die.'

'"Have some of my chobbal," I said. "No," you said. "I'm going to get my revenge on that boss-eyed skink," you said. "That will teach him to bite me," you said. Not feeling so clever now, are you?'

'*Zorki*, Aisha, can't a man even throw up without his wife nagging him?'

'Fine. If my sympathy is wasted on you, I'll go back to bed.'

Sophie listened to the woman's retreating footsteps and waited for Usman to go in as well. She hoped desperately that he would not notice the hole further along the fence.

Usman stayed outside for a few minutes, muttering to himself, but he seemed to have emptied his stomach because there was no more vomiting. At last Sophie heard him return to his tent. She lay quietly for a while longer and then she took a deep breath and stood up.

As quickly and quietly as she could, Sophie climbed into Chobbal's saddle and crossed her feet gently in the U of his neck. His back legs unfolded slowly, rocking her forward, and then the front legs, lifting her up into the air. She picked up the reins, kicked his side gently and guided him over to the gap in the thorns. A large brown one-eyed camel stood up and snorted at them as they passed.

Through the gap they went, and out into the open.

Sophie did not want to linger in the camp, but she could not venture into the desert without water. She guided Chobbal over to the well and looked down into it. A faint glimmer of moonlight reflected off the water far away beneath her.

On the brick wall around the well, just within Sophie's reach, were a bucket and a coil of thick rope. She picked up one end of the rope and tied it carefully around Chobbal's hump. She tied the other end to the handle of the bucket. Not long now.

Sophie had just begun to lower the bucket when she heard a sound behind her. It was the one sound which she dreaded more than any other sound in the world – even more than the hiss of a snake.

What Sophie heard was the jingle-jangle of a tiny bell.

Chapter 11

'*Salam alaykum*, white girl. Did you pass the night in peace?'

Sophie turned round. The one-eyed camel stood behind her, and sitting on the camel was a man. He wore a big blue turban and on a ribbon round his neck hung a silver bell. Sophie found herself looking at the hollow cheeks and glittering black eyes of the most feared bandit in the Sahara Desert, Moussa ag Litni.

Ag Litni smiled crookedly. 'Ooh,' he said, 'I love it when I get visitors.'

Sophie let go of the bucket, which fell away into the darkness and landed with an echoing splash. With shaking fingers, she fumbled to untie the rope around Chobbal's hump.

'Can I help you with that?' said ag Litni.

The rope came loose and Sophie kicked Chobbal's flank with both heels. He started to walk.

Ag Litni brought his camel alongside her, so close that the saddles were almost touching.

'We are simple folk,' he said, 'but we like to honour our visitors. Would you prefer your coffin to be made of baobab or calabash wood?'

Sophie opened her mouth to scream but nothing came out. She kicked the camel's flank again, harder this time. How could Chobbal not understand? Surely he realised how evil this man was. Surely he could sense her fear. Come on now, think. *What did Gidaado say to make Chobbal run?*

'*Kaboosh*,' she croaked. Tears welled up in her eyes.

'I'm sorry,' said Moussa ag Litni, cupping his hand over his ear and grinning across at her. 'What did you say?'

'*Babooshka!*' Sophie cried.

'You will have to speak Fulfulde or Tamacheq,' said Moussa ag Litni, stroking his long black beard. 'I do not understand much Russian.'

'*Foosh-ka!*' squeaked Sophie. Chobbal turned his head and raised an eyebrow.

'It has been nice talking to you,' said Moussa ag Litni, 'but you are beginning to bore me. I have a sudden desire to dance.' He took a long silver knife from his belt, and raised it above his head.

Sophie stared at the knife. '*Moosh-ka!*' she shouted.

The knife started to come down, and then Sophie remembered.

'*HOOSH-KA!*' she screamed.

Chobbal broke into a run and ag Litni slashed the air inches behind Sophie.

'Oooh,' said Moussa ag Litni. 'We have a chase! *HOOSH-KA!*'

*

Sophie held on to the reins tightly as Chobbal galloped off into the dunes. Her mind was spinning with fear and confusion. Behind her she could hear ag Litni's wild laughter and the hooves of his camel, but she dared not look back to see how close he was.

'You can run,' ag Litni shouted, 'but in the desert there is *nowhere to hide*!'

Nowhere to hide. How could she possibly escape? Sophie could hear her own pulse pounding in her ears, *DUM BABA-DUM BABA-DUM BABA-DUM BABA-DUM. Alai was a little boy Alai was only eight he had a buck-toothed camel they were the best of mates. Ag Litni always wins. Ag Litni always wins. Ag Litni always wins.*

But beyond Sophie's terror there was a still, small voice. *Think, Sophie. You must calm down and think.*

She thought. To run further north into the desert would be senseless. If there was any hope for her, it lay towards the south – towards Gidaado and Gorom-Gorom. But which way *was* south? Sophie looked around her – nothing but shifting sand and shadowy acacia bushes.

Then she saw it. Far away in front of her there was a faint glow on the horizon. The sun was about to rise! If the sun was going to rise in front of her, that meant she was travelling east. So to go south she needed to turn right. No, left. No, right.

Sophie yanked Chobbal's reins to the right. Another peal of laughter rang out behind her.

'Where are you going?' yelled ag Litni. 'Must you leave already? We have not yet had our Dance!'

'HOOSH-BARAKAAA!' cried Sophie. Chobbal lowered his head and his ears went back. He was really flying now.

'HOOSH-BARAKAAA!' cried ag Litni behind her. 'I love a little run before breakfast, don't you?'

Ag Litni's taunts were making Sophie angry.

'Boil your head!' she yelled. It was not very imaginative, but it was the best she could think of.

'*Zorki*,' said the Tuareg. 'A white girl who speaks Fulfulde. How intelligent you are, my dear. Rude, but intelligent.'

81

'You will never catch me!' yelled Sophie. 'You should give up now.'

More cackles of wild laughter. 'The albino is fast, I grant you,' shouted ag Litni, 'but he will tire soon. Nyiiri here may only have one eye but he is my best chaser – the finest long-distance runner in the Sahara. He can run for six hours if he has a full stomach.'

'And does he have a full stomach now?'

'Guess!' cried ag Litni, and he whooped maniacally.

So Gidaado had been right. *Moussa ag Litni knows that his chasers have enough stamina to keep going for as long as it takes. Sooner or later his victim's camel will get tired and stop. Ag Litni always wins.*

The sun was rising in the east and the sky was getting lighter. It was now possible to see the sandy ground ahead, stretching away towards the flat horizon. The sun was still on Sophie's left, so she knew she was heading in the right direction.

With Chobbal charging along so fast, it was all

Sophie could do not to fall off. She held on to the upright prong of the camel's saddle and tried to grip his sides with her knees. How long had they been running? And how much longer would it be until Chobbal got tired and slowed down?

Far away in the distance there was a tiny dark shape on the horizon. An acacia bush? No, it was the wrong shape for that. It was roundish, like a hut. Of course! This must be the settlement they had passed last night. Sophie tweaked the reins slightly to the left and headed straight for it.

'Don't get your hopes up,' shouted ag Litni behind her. 'The family which owns that hut only uses it occasionally. And even if they are there, they will run away as soon as they see me. I usually have that effect on people.'

On and on they galloped. Sophie's hair streamed out behind her and the thunder of camel hooves filled her ears. The hut looked closer now, but it was still a long way away. Besides, Sophie knew that there was no one in the hut except a very angry cobra wearing a yellow shirt. *Gidaado*, she thought, *where are you?*

'HOOSH-BARAKAAAAAAA,' cried ag Litni. 'What an exciting chase! But I fear it is going to end soon.'

Sophie did not want to admit it but Chobbal *was* beginning to get tired. She was not being shaken around as much as before, and the sound of Nyiiri's hooves behind her was louder than ever. It was terrible but true – Chobbal was slowing down. He would slow to a trot and he would stop and that would be the end of it. The end of her. *Think, Sophie.* That voice in her head again. *You must calm down and think.*

Sophie studied the landscape in front of her, trying to recognise something, anything, from the night before. There was a forked tree Sophie remembered passing. And farther away there was a large flat stone she thought she recognised. She tweaked the reins slightly to the left and cantered on.

Ag Litni was right on her tail, now. 'Well done, Nyiiri,' he was saying. 'You have done it again. It is moments like this that make all the training worthwhile, is it not?'

About fifty metres ahead, Sophie noticed a

small, oddly-shaped hump of sand. She tweaked the reins again slightly. Left a bit, left a bit more. She was thinking furiously. There was one particular word she was trying to remember – a word that might just save her life.

Sophie glanced behind and saw that ag Litni was so close he could almost touch her. He was brandishing his silver knife and shaking his head and arms violently. It was the beginning of the Death Dance.

'*Oooooh, eeee, ooh-ah-ah*,' sang Moussa ag Litni in ghoulish ecstasy.

Twenty metres, fifteen, ten . . .

The odd-shaped hump of sand shuddered and stood up and there before them, covered in sand, stood Gidaado the Fourth. He was standing right in the path of the camels with one hand in his pocket and the other pointing down at the ground in front of him. Sophie bit her lip and tweaked the reins to the left. She would only have one chance to get this right.

'BAHAAT-UGH!!!!!!!' yelled Sophie and pulled back on the reins with all her might. Chobbal dug his front hooves into the ground and skidded to a halt, throwing up dust and sand all around.

'BAHAAT-UGH!!!!!!!' yelled Moussa ag Litni, and he skidded to a halt alongside Sophie, grinning horribly from ear to ear, his knife looming high in the air. Then his grin turned to an expression of complete astonishment as he and his camel disappeared through the ground.

A huge cloud of dust billowed up from the abyss. Sophie blinked and shielded her eyes. Chobbal snorted in alarm and tiptoed backwards away from the hole. As the dust settled, the children stood still and listened. From somewhere underground came the muffled but very angry voice of Moussa ag Litni, the most evil man in West Africa.

'Zorki!' said the voice. 'Zorki zorki zorki zorki ZORKI!'

Gidaado shook his head sadly. 'Look at that hole,' he said. 'It's incredibly dangerous.'

'Someone should put a big sign next to it,' said Sophie.

Chapter 12

It was nine o'clock in the morning by the time they arrived at Gidaado's village. Gidaado knocked on the door of the square hut, and a little old woman opened it and peered out at them. She had great long earlobes and her skin was as wrinkly as a baobab fruit.

'You half-witted son of a skink!' she said, glaring at Gidaado. 'You no-good dollop of *dordi*. Why have you woken me up? I'm a very sick woman. And you're eighteen and a half hours late. Here am I waiting for my medicine from Gorom-Gorom and you go and stay in town the whole day and the whole night, singing your daft songs and dancing your daft dances and not sparing a thought for your old grandmother lying in bed waiting for her medicine.'

'Sorry, Grandmother.'

'Well it's nice to see you. And the white girl too, whoever she is. Go and light the fire, Gidaado, and I'll fetch some coffee beans.'

'I've twisted my ankle, Grandmother.'

'That's nice,' said the old woman.

'And Moussa ag Litni has fallen into a disused well about three hours' ride north-west of here.'

'That's nice,' said the old woman again, disappearing into the hut.

Half an hour later, Gidaado and Sophie were sitting on a millet stalk mat in the shade behind the hut. Nearby, a cauldron of coffee was balanced on two logs, the fire underneath it burning fiercely. Gidaado's grandmother had pounded the coffee beans herself in a big wooden mortar, along with some black pepper to give the coffee an extra kick. She had even added some *barka* leaves, which she claimed would heal Gidaado's ankle. The smoke from the fire made Sophie's eyes sting whenever the wind blew in her direction.

'My grandmother has gone to fetch Uncle Ibrahiim from the field,' said Gidaado. 'When he comes he will take you home on his motorbike.'

Sophie looked away and swallowed hard. It would be wonderful to see Dad again. She imagined arriving home and seeing her father sitting in front of his desert flytrap with his head in his hands. She imagined the look on his face when he noticed her standing in the doorway, the tears in his eyes and the smell of earth and pollen on his shirt-front when he hugged her to him. She would say a little speech about how wrong she had been to go off without telling him, and he would say, 'I'm just glad you're okay, darling.' And then his glasses would steam up and he would start wagging his finger and lecturing her about Fatimata Tamboura. 'Never mess with the Sahara Desert,' he would say, and she would promise to try harder in future. It would be good to be home.

'You're crying,' said Gidaado.

'I'm not,' said Sophie. 'It's the smoke in my eyes.'

Gidaado clicked his tongue dubiously.

'Wait, that's it,' said Sophie.

'What?'

'Smoke. Goes away and never comes back.'

'Go on,' said Gidaado.

Sophie looked over at Chobbal, who was busy chewing on the corner of the millet stalk mat, and then she turned back to Gidaado. 'I am Fire,' she said. 'My sons are Smoke, Flame and Ash. Smoke goes away but never comes back. Flame eats but is never full. Ash falls down but never gets up.'

Gidaado clapped his hands. 'Excellent,' he said. 'You are almost as intelligent as a griot.'

Sophie chuckled. 'Ask me another,' she said.

9

"Sure!" Jenny said after a slight pause. "In fact, I'm on my way over to the tack shop in Willow Creek, so I can give you a ride. Where are you?"

"I'm at Pine Hollow," Carole said.

"Perfect. I know just where that is."

"I'll wait at the end of the driveway. It'll be easier that way," Carole added hastily.

The moment the call ended, she grabbed her things from the locker room and trudged out to the road. She knew it would take Jenny half an hour to get there, but she didn't want to wait around Pine Hollow. She didn't want to answer questions about where she was going—or why.

"I'm so glad you changed your mind!" said Jenny when she pulled up in a white pickup. "Hop in—and watch out for all the tack. I just had a bunch of stuff repaired.

"You know, I meant what I said about you and King," the older girl continued once they were on the way. "You're a good rider, and you and he could go far."

"Thanks," Carole mumbled, embarrassed by two things: one, the compliment, and two, the fact that Jenny seemed to think she was seriously considering buying King. And why wouldn't she? Carole had said nothing to reveal the true situation: that though she could never, ever afford King, she longed to ride him again.

"Have you ever thought of doing top-level dressage?"

Carole swallowed. She nodded.

"Well, then, King is your horse," Jenny replied.

"I—I would probably still ride in Pony Club events and other shows," Carole said hesitantly, "I mean, for *fun* . . ."

Jenny gave her a smile. "You really think so? I'll tell you, when I started riding dressage—I mean for real, none of this backyard stuff—I never looked back. Carole, every rider has to choose sometime. Every great rider, that is."

Carole shifted uncomfortably in her seat. *She* did "backyard stuff." On the other hand, she knew Jenny was right about the need to specialize. If you looked at the Olympics or any of the top international competitions, all the riders did one thing and one thing only. Some were show jumpers, jumping high, technical courses in a ring. Others rode at the highest levels of dressage.

"There is three-day eventing," Carole said aloud. Eventing, or combined training, was a sport that combined dressage and jumping. The first phase was dressage, the second was a cross-country jumping course, and the third was stadium jumping (not unlike show jumping) in a ring.

"That's true," Jenny said, sounding unconvinced. "But their dressage is nowhere near as good as ours, and for all I know, their jumping isn't, either. I guess if you want an all-around sport . . ." she added doubtfully. "Do you?"

Carole looked out the window before answering. The problem was, she didn't know what she wanted. All her life people had been telling her she was talented. Nobody had told her in which direction to take her talent. "I don't know," she said finally. "I just don't know."

JENNY HAD TO get some paperwork done before her first lesson, so after bringing King in from the pasture, she told Carole to make herself at home and ride wherever she liked. "There's a trail that makes a loop beside the pasture," she suggested.

Carole tacked up and led King out to the ring. When she mounted, she had the same incredible feeling as be-

89

fore. She felt privileged just to be sitting on his back. It reminded her of when she was little and used to go to big horse shows as a spectator. Once in a while, one of the competitors would give her a ride. King felt as special as those horses.

Carole warmed him up slowly, taking her time. "Imagine if I brought you to a dressage lesson!" she murmured. "Max wouldn't be able to find a single thing wrong with us!" Carole walked and trotted. Even a simple exercise like trotting a circle was a joy. Then she pretended she was riding a grand prix dressage show. She trotted down the center line of the ring to an imaginary X—the center point. There she halted, took off her hat, and saluted the imaginary judge. Starlight was usually difficult to keep in place during the salute. He was impatient, ready to be off across the cross-country fields. But King stood rock solid. One ear moved back, asking for Carole's next request.

"You're so perfect, I don't know what to do with you!" she said, laughing. Remembering Max's advice to keep things interesting, Carole spied the set of cavalletti at the end of the ring. They were still in place from Pat's ride. Carole turned King toward them. This time around, instead of avoiding them, she urged the horse over them. King's ears went forward. Carole tensed in the saddle, waiting for the takeoff over the first jump. But King moved unsteadily, weaving from side to side. At the last minute he half jumped, half stumbled over the obstacle, falling heavily against the bit.

Her stomach turning over, Carole felt the wrench against the reins. She was so embarrassed she glanced involuntarily toward the house, praying that Jenny had not seen. Here Jenny had trusted Carole with her extremely valuable horse, and Carole was messing up his training. Obviously she hadn't prepared him correctly for the jump. Horse sense told Carole she should go around again, but she didn't want to. She was too afraid of doing something wrong. With Starlight, over fences, she was used to just sitting tight, head up, heels down, and checking him when he got too strong. A horse like King probably expected a lot more precision, guidance, and control.

"Let's just take a nice trail ride, why don't we?" Carole said, giving the brown neck a long pat. She loosened the reins and headed out of the pasture.

It was a magical ride. The winter sun had finally come out. It glinted on King's rich coat and shone through the trees. King walked and jogged comfortably. True to his warmblood breeding, he was powerful but steady. Alone in the quiet of the woods, Carole could almost pretend that King was hers. *She* could be the "right rider" to go "all the way"—maybe even to the Olympics! With a horse like King, she could be a junior dressage *star*. Imagine Max's face—imagine Stevie, Lisa, her father, Mrs. Reg—when she got chosen for the team!

Lost in her daydream, Carole didn't see the fallen log in the path. She was trotting along when all of a sudden King stopped dead. Carole was thrown forward onto his neck. A wave of fear washed over her. Why had King stopped? If something had happened to him . . . Then she saw the log and let out a sigh of relief. "It's only a tree, silly boy!" she said. "Come on, over you go!" She clucked to him and used her legs, but King did not want to move forward. He did not want to step over the log. Suddenly Carole was afraid again. What if he knew something about this trail that she didn't? Could there be danger on the other side? Feeling nervous and unsettled, she turned King around and headed back the way she'd come. She certainly wasn't going to take any chances.

The ride back to Jenny's was no fun at all. Carole dreaded telling Jenny the truth—that she adored King, thought he was perfect, but couldn't afford him in a million years. She felt sick with anxiety. Jenny was a professional. She wanted to sell King. She wouldn't be pleased to hear that Carole had been riding with no intention to buy.

In the time left, Carole composed her speech. When

King was untacked and put away, she walked up to the house. Her palms sweaty, she knocked on the door.

"Come in! I'm in back!"

"King is probably the best horse I've ever ridden," Carole said to herself, rehearsing. She found Jenny in her office.

"Up to my elbows in bills!" Jenny said cheerfully. "How'd it go? Did you try any airs above the ground?"

Carole tried to smile. She tried to speak, but the words stuck in her throat. Her feet seemed rooted to the floor. "I—" Then all at once, forgetting her speech entirely, she blurted out, "I love King but I can't afford him! I'll never be able to afford him!"

"But Carole—"

Carole rushed on before Jenny could get upset with her. "I couldn't resist the chance to ride him again, but I—I have a horse already and my dad and I could never afford another and even if we could he wouldn't let me have two horses and—and—I hope you're not mad!" she finished with a convulsive sob.

Jenny stood up and put an arm around Carole's shaking shoulders. "Of course I'm not mad!" she said. "I was happy to have you ride King. But sweetie, there's a solution to your problem."

Carole raised a tearstained face. "There is?"

Jenny laughed. "Boy, are you silly! You don't even see

the answer and it's staring you in the face. What's your horse like?"

"Starlight?" Carole said, confused.

"Yes. Tell me about him."

Carole sniffed. "He's—He's great," she began falteringly. "He's half Thoroughbred. He's won a lot—I mean, not at the biggest shows, but he's won a lot of Pony Club events and been champion at local shows. He's a great jumper. I—I trained him myself," Carole added.

"So in other words, Starlight is a very successful children's hunter with a show record to match. He's probably worth a lot—a lot more than you know, even."

"I guess," Carole said, frowning. She couldn't understand what Jenny was getting at.

"Well, then, Carole," Jenny concluded, beaming. "It's simple: Sell Starlight!"

CAROLE SAT AT the dinner table, listlessly toying with her food. She could feel her father's eyes on her. She took a bite of chicken and chewed it methodically. By drinking half a glass of water, she managed to get it down.

"If you don't like the rations, you can tell the cook, you know, honey," said Colonel Hanson, his dark eyes twinkling.

Carole looked up, her face stricken. "It's not that, Dad! It's good—really."

94

"Then how about telling me what's wrong? You've been brooding since you walked in the door."

Carole sighed. She looked down at her plate again. "Dad, what would you do if you had a huge decision to make?"

Colonel Hanson put his knife and fork down and wiped his mouth. He thought seriously. "First of all, I wouldn't rush it, Carole. I'd—"

"Oh, Dad, you're right!" cried Carole.

Her father raised his eyebrows. "You mean that's all I had to say?"

Carole half smiled. "For now, anyway. You see, if I did anything about this . . . this decision, it would take me a long time to put it into action, you see, because it's not easy to sell—I mean, it takes a long time to find—well, you know what I mean."

"Not exactly," Colonel Hanson said, laughing, "but I'll trust you on that. Now how about my chicken tetrazzini?"

"I just got my appetite back!" As Carole picked up her fork, the doorbell rang. Colonel Hanson went to get it.

Carole sighed with relief. She didn't have to decide anything now. It could take weeks—months—to sell Starlight. *Sell Starlight.* Even the phrase made Carole shudder. She wasn't going to think about it. She'd just block it out. Tomorrow she would call Jenny to see if she could ride King a few more times. After all, that was completely normal. Buyers often rode the horses they were interested in five, even six times. Carole's dream of riding grand prix dressage came flooding back to her. If she chose to specialize in dressage now, at this young age, she'd be miles ahead of everyone.

Suddenly it came to her: She could write a story about a horse like King for the *Horseman's Weekly* contest! A champion dressage horse shown by a junior rider—a girl, of course, just like Carole. Maybe she'd win the contest, too! Maybe she'd—

"Carole! Some friends of yours are here!" her father called.

Carole got up and went out to the hallway, thinking, *Stevie and Lisa must have been wondering where I was.* As she walked to the door, her gaze flew up to the picture of The Saddle Club. It hung right next to her school portraits. The three of them were all riding the horses they had ridden not long after they'd met. Suddenly Carole felt a chill. Which horse would she be riding in the next picture of The Saddle Club? Putting the decision off was only a temporary solution—which meant it was no solution, really.

Distracted, Carole turned the hall corner. She stopped in surprise. "Pat! Hello!" she cried. "Gosh, I was expecting you to be Stevie and Lisa!"

"Sorry we're not The Saddle Club," said Pat. She gestured to the well-dressed man beside her. "Meet my husband, Dave."

Carole shook hands with Mr. Naughton. He looked as nice as she had expected.

"It's great to meet you, Carole," he said. "I've heard so much about you—and Starlight."

"Why don't you both come in for coffee?" Colonel Hanson said. "We're just finishing dinner and we'd enjoy the company, wouldn't we, Carole?"

"Definitely, Dad."

"Thanks so much," said Pat, "but I'm afraid we can't stay. Our daughter is at home with the baby-sitter."

"And the baby-sitter will have our heads if we're late," Dave explained. "Confidentially, I think she's got a date," he whispered.

The four laughed. Pat cleared her throat. "Carole, I should get right to the point."

Carole looked up, surprised that there *was* a point. She'd assumed the Naughtons had simply stopped by on a friendly visit. When Pat spoke, Carole noticed that she seemed excited and a bit nervous.

"We were driving home from dinner and I was telling Dave about how much fun we've been having and—and also about how much I enjoyed riding Starlight." Pat paused. She seemed to be choosing her words carefully. "I've been looking for a horse for several months now. I know what's out there, and, well"—she glanced at her husband—"Carole, we just had the craziest idea."

"My wife didn't want to say anything, but I insisted," Dave said. "I said you never know until you try. Carole, Colonel Hanson: We'd like to make an offer on Starlight."

Carole stared unthinkingly as Pat hurried on. "Now, I know it's crazy, Carole. And totally pointless. But Dave did think we ought to at least mention the idea to you. I know you said someday you'd want to move on, and—and if that day is soon, well, I think Starlight is just wonderful. I'd give him a great home—right at Pine Hollow, in fact. You could see him every day, ride him whenever you wanted . . ."

Out of the corner of her eye, Carole could see the perplexed expression on her father's face. She didn't know what to say. She just stood there, looking at the Naughtons, her mouth dry.

"As for price," Dave continued, "Pat knows horses and I know finance. I don't know what you paid for Starlight, but my wife tells me you've trained him and showed him and made him what he is today. We talked about it, and I hope this won't be an insult." Dave took a breath and named a sum.

Carole's jaw dropped. The offer was double what she

would have expected. She put a hand on the wall to steady herself.

Dimly she was aware of the phone ringing and her father excusing himself to answer it.

Carole sat down on the hall stairs.

"I know we're throwing this at you," Pat said apologetically. "And you don't have to decide now, of course. But if you think you'd even consider the offer, you know where to find me."

Carole nodded. "Sure, Pat." Something told her to stand up. She stood up. Something told her to go through the motions of shaking hands with Pat and Dave.

"See you at Pine Hollow," Pat said warmly.

"Yeah, see you at Pine Hollow," Carole repeated. She closed the door behind them. Her mind was reeling but at the same time blank. Finally a thought crystallized. She almost hated to admit it was there. The Naughtons' offer sounded huge. But at the back of her mind she was wondering how much more Jenny would want for King.

Her father's voice broke the silence. "It's Stevie and Lisa, Carole!" he called. When Carole didn't answer, he came out into the hall. "Sweetheart?"

Carole raised her eyes slowly. "Will you take a message, Dad?" she whispered. "I just can't talk to them right now."

CAROLE FELL INTO bed, exhausted. She craved sleep. She didn't want to think. She wanted to block everything out. But once she got into bed, she was wide awake. She stared at the ceiling, counting the minutes.

Her brain seemed to be stuck on instant replay. First she saw the girl Missy with her pony, explaining, "I don't want to sell him at all. But I'm getting a new horse in two weeks . . ." Then her mind flashed to Pat admitting, "I've never been on that side of the fence" and asking Carole if she'd ever sold a horse. But Jenny's words were loudest, repeating themselves, echoing in her mind. "It's time to move on. I've taken him as far as I can. . . . *You're* not looking, are you?" And again: "It's time to

100

move on. . . . Too bad. You'd make a great pair. . . . Too bad. You'd make a great pair. . . ."

Carole tossed and turned. She would feel sleep coming on, then would suddenly sit bolt upright in bed. Maybe the reason she couldn't do anything with Starlight lately was that it *was* time to move on. Maybe she had taken Starlight as far as she could. Maybe it was time to let someone else ride him. There was no doubt that King's Ransom was her big chance to go from local competitions to national—or even international.

Carole looked longingly at the telephone. She desperately wanted to call Stevie and Lisa now, but it was much too late. They wouldn't understand, anyway. They'd want to know why Starlight and the Pony Club weren't good enough for her. They'd remind her about Briarwood and other big shows at which she had ridden. Most of all, they wouldn't understand the need to specialize in dressage. The truth was, Carole thought, Stevie's and Lisa's dreams about riding weren't as big as hers. For them, riding was a great sport, not an all-consuming passion. But Carole couldn't explain that to them.

There was someone who would understand, though: Jenny. She would understand perfectly. She had been through it all herself. Resolving to call King's owner the next day, Carole turned the light off. Then she turned the light back on. She didn't care how late it was. She had to call Jenny right then. She dialed the number and listened anxiously. After a couple of rings Jenny picked up, sounding sleepy.

"I'm sorry," Carole said urgently. "I know it's too late to call."

"That's okay. What's up?" asked Jenny.

"I—I think I might have the money for King!" Carole said hurriedly. "Or at least part of it."

"Really?" said Jenny, after a pause. "So you've come to a decision?"

"No—Yes—I don't know. But somebody made an offer on Starlight tonight. I think you're right. I think I do want to concentrate on dressage."

"Carole, that's great!" Jenny exclaimed. "See? I knew you could figure it out if you tried. How much did they offer?"

"What?"

"How much was the offer for Starlight?"

"Oh," said Carole. She was a little surprised that Jenny had mentioned price so soon. But, after all, Carole reminded herself, Jenny was a professional. There was no point in pretending that money didn't matter. It did. Period.

"That's a great start!" Jenny said enthusiastically when Carole told her the offer. "You could pay me the rest over the next year."

"Oh. Right." Carole's hands suddenly felt clammy. How could she tell Jenny she had no way of earning the rest? She would simply have to figure something out. To be a world-famous junior rider, she would have to make sacrifices. She could work after school, weekends—two jobs, if need be . . .

"Come ride King on Monday morning and we'll firm things up," Jenny said. "Maybe you could bring a deposit then."

Feeling slightly sick, Carole explained that school started on Monday.

"All right, then, Monday afternoon."

All at once Carole regretted making the phone call. Things were happening too fast. She was sure her decision was the right one, but she needed more time to let it sink in. "How about if I come next Friday?" she asked nervously, stalling for time.

The tone of Jenny's voice changed ever so slightly. "All right. I guess that's okay. But Carole, you do understand that until I get a commitment from you—a financial commitment—I'm going to keep showing King to buyers. There are a number of people who are interested in him."

"Sure," said Carole, "I understand." She got off the phone as quickly fast as she could and lay back on her pillows. *I ought to turn the light off,* she thought, just before falling into a troubled sleep.

* * *

FOR THE FIRST time ever, Carole was glad to go back to school on Monday. She didn't hate school the way Stevie did, but she didn't love it, either, like Lisa. To Carole, school was just there—a place she had to go five days a week until she was old enough to turn professional and ride full-time. But now it seemed like an escape, a distraction from the announcement she was going to make on Friday.

But even in school, the decision haunted her. She hadn't been to Pine Hollow once since the jumping fiasco. And now she certainly couldn't go. How could she ride Starlight, groom him, fuss over him, when all the while she was planning to sell him?

At least he was getting exercise, Carole thought sadly, picking at her food in the cafeteria one afternoon. Knowing she couldn't face riding, she had told Pat she could take Starlight out. Pat, of course, had been thrilled. "Really, Carole?" she'd said. The happiness in Pat's voice made Carole sad, too. Clearly Pat deserved Starlight— unlike Carole, who spent every moment dreaming about King.

The bell rang; lunch period was over. Carole stood up quickly and bused her tray. Lisa had spent lunch in the library, but Carole didn't want to risk running into her. Lisa would ask her a lot of questions. "Why haven't you been riding?" "Why haven't you been helping out with barn chores?" "What are you going to do for your demonstration for Max?"

After lunch, Carole had English. The class was doing a unit on creative writing. "I want you all to write a story and hand it in on Monday," the teacher announced. "You can write on anything you want, but my suggestion is simple: Write about what you know."

The story! Carole remembered suddenly. In her dilemma, she had forgotten all about the *Horseman's Weekly* contest. *At least now I'll have something to write about,* she thought ruefully. Instead of a champion junior rider, she would write about a girl who had to sell her horse. It would be a sad story but a good one. Carole looked down at her notebook, feeling her eyes fill up with tears. Why was doing the right thing so hard—and so sad?

Carole sniffed. If she let herself go, she would burst out crying for real, and she hated to cry in school. She frowned and opened her assignment book. By Friday it would all be over. Starlight would belong to someone else. Across Saturday and Sunday Carole wrote, in big black letters, "Write story!" One story could work for English class and for the contest.

The teacher told the students to take ten minutes to work on their opening sentences. *How should the story start?* Carole wondered. She knew how it would end. The final sentence would be easy: *The day she sold her first horse was the saddest day of her life.*

"COME ON! COME on! Come on!"

Stevie sprinted up the driveway toward Lisa. She ran flat out for the house. "Home!" she cried, tagging the front door.

Lisa clicked the stopwatch. "Your best time ever!"

"All right, twenty sit-ups and I'll be done," said Stevie. Inside she dropped to the floor and did her crunches. Stevie, who went to Fenton Hall, a private school, had an extra week of vacation, so Lisa had put her on a schedule. Mornings she did the abs and arms video by herself. Afternoons Lisa came by to time her runs.

Even Stevie had to admit that the plan had worked. After two solid weeks of exercise, she was ready. Mid-crunch, Alex poked his head into the family room.

"Aren't you going to taper off before the competition?" he asked, sounding worried. "It *is* tomorrow, you know— unless you need more time, of course."

Stevie grinned. "Eighteen. Nineteen. Twenty. Phew!" She sat up. "You know, Lisa," she said, "it's sad to see a grown man cry. But what's even sadder is to see a half-grown man who's scared of a couple of girls!"

Alex made a face at her and retreated. Giggling, Stevie collapsed on the couch next to Lisa. "I bet we'll be about even in the race," she mused. Then she sat up. "Darn! I wish there was some contest where *I'd* have the upper hand. I know he'll beat me in push-ups, just because he's a boy."

Lisa concentrated. "I'll try to think of something," she promised.

"How's school?" Stevie asked suddenly. Not looking forward to Monday, she needed all the encouragement she could get.

"Great!" said Lisa.

"You always say that."

"No, but it is great. In fact, everything's great. I get my homework done on time, I'm *ahead* in two classes, I do my chores right away, I'm two-thirds through my needle-point—"

"I know what you mean," said Stevie. "I'm sticking to this fitness program, I've done all my laundry down to the last unmatched sock, I've watched *Priced to Sell* every afternoon and made dessert every night—"

Stevie stopped. The two girls looked at each other. Then they both looked at the floor. "So you haven't been . . . uh . . . ," Stevie began.

"No. You?"

"No."

"Well, so what!" Lisa said. "We *always* help with barn chores."

107

"That's right!" agreed Stevie. "Maybe it was time for someone else to take up the slack."

"Yeah! And realize that The Saddle Club isn't going to do *all* the dirty work!"

"And—And I'm sure Red's been turning Belle out in the pasture," Stevie said more quietly.

"And I'll bet somebody else has been riding Prancer," Lisa added in a small voice.

"And—And I'm sure that Carole still wants to be our friend," Stevie added, her voice doleful.

Lisa swallowed. "I'm positive Carole's not mad at us."

"I'll bet if Carole's at Pine Hollow right now—" Stevie faltered, her voice trembling.

"She—She probably misses us . . ."

"So what if we skipped two weeks?" Stevie said defensively.

"It doesn't mean we're bad people!" Lisa cried.

"Or that we'll never be welcome at Pine Hollow again!" Stevie wailed.

"Or that Mrs. Reg hates us!"

"Or that The Saddle Club is over!"

That did it. Lisa stood up. She gave Stevie a hand and pulled her up from the couch. The two girls got their coats from the hall closet. They grabbed their gloves and ran down the driveway. When they got to the road, they turned left and raced for Pine Hollow. "I hope it's not too late!" Lisa shouted.

"It won't be!" answered Stevie. "Not with the shape we're in!"

FIVE MINUTES LATER the two girls stormed into Pine Hollow. For some reason, both of them expected a trumpet to blow, signaling their return. But the barn was as quiet as it normally was on a winter Friday. Stevie looked into Belle's stall. It was empty.

"Oh, I turned her out this morning," said Red when Stevie found him. "She's out playing in the pasture."

Lisa searched for Prancer. As a last resort, she checked the indoor ring. Andrea Barry was riding the mare in place of her own horse. "Oh, I didn't know you were coming. Doc's a little off his feed, so I've been practicing on Prancer," the girl said. "I hope it's okay."

"Okay?" said Lisa. "It's the best!" Andrea was an excellent rider. Any schooling from her could only benefit Prancer. Lisa headed for the tack room.

Stevie was already there. "What on earth?" Stevie's saddle and bridle were gleaming. So were Lisa's.

"Carole!" Lisa exclaimed.

"Naturally!"

Mrs. Reg peeked in to say hi.

"Do you know where Carole is?" Stevie asked breathlessly.

"Gosh, no. I haven't seen in her in over a week," Mrs. Reg replied. "Pat Naughton's been exercising Starlight, though. You could ask her."

"Over a week!" Lisa exclaimed. She was stunned. Stevie was flabbergasted. That simply could not be. It was one thing for them to skip a week of riding, but *Carole*? They left the tack room and hurried down the aisle to Starlight's stall.

Pat Naughton had the gelding out on cross-ties and was grooming him. "Good boy!" She straightened up from picking out a hoof. "Well, hello!"

"Mrs. Naughton?" Stevie said after introducing Lisa. "Is it true that Carole hasn't been coming to ride?"

"Call me Pat, and yes, I'm afraid it is. She said something about having too much homework, so I've been exercising Starlight. Not every day, just occasionally."

Lisa stared. Stevie stared. Neither of them had to say

what they were both thinking: Even if her teachers had given her fifty hours of homework a night, Carole would never have skipped riding. Something was up. Something serious.

"Let's go call her. *Now*," said Lisa.

"I don't think you'll need to," Pat said. She pointed down the aisle. "Here she comes."

Carole stopped in her tracks when she saw Stevie and Lisa. Then she continued toward them. Why not tell everyone all at once and get it over with? She heard Mrs. Reg coming up behind her. "Even better," Carole murmured.

Starlight pricked up his ears when he saw his owner coming. He nickered softly. Gritting her teeth, Carole stopped before the small crowd and said, "I have an announcement to make. I've made a decision."

Bubbly as ever, Pat Naughton did not seem to understand the gravity of the situation. "Carole!" she cried. "Welcome back. Starlight missed you so much. He's been playing me up like crazy."

"How do you guys know each other?" Stevie asked, curious about the new friendship between one of her neighbors and one of her best friends.

"Carole's been helping me look for a horse," Pat explained. "We saw one amazing horse—King's Ransom—didn't we, Carole?"

"Yes," said Carole, feeling sick but determined to break the news. "In fact, that's what—"

"Only one thing wrong with him!" Pat said, giggling. "He couldn't jump a stick! Remember when I tried those tiny jumps and he stumbled all over them? Practically fell on his face!"

Carole looked quickly at Pat. "What did you say?"

"*You* know—when I tried to jump! Oh, no, that's right, you were in the bathroom, weren't you? But gosh, this horse was a joke over fences!"

"I know that horse," put in Mrs. Reg. "Girl went over to Holland and brought back an event horse. Or so she thought. Turned out he couldn't jump. Crashed through half a dozen courses. They turned him into a dressage horse. He does fairly well—"

"Ick!" said Stevie. "Who would want to do dressage all the time?"

"A lot of people," Carole said defensively.

"I guess," Stevie conceded. "Sounds boring to me. No Pony Club, no hunting, no trail riding—although I guess this horse could probably jump all right on the trail. *Any* horse can jump outside."

Carole felt herself flush. King had refused to jump the log on the trail! "I—I was thinking of buying King!" she blurted out.

Stevie, Lisa, Pat, and Mrs. Reg all looked at her. Carole

113

waited for them to express their shock. Instead they started to laugh. They seemed to think she was joking, or only half serious. "You? Give up jumping? Yeah, right!" said Stevie. "And I'll give up hating school!"

"If you gave up jumping, who would represent The Saddle Club in the American Horse Show? I mean, when we're in high school?" Lisa asked.

Only Mrs. Reg was serious. "Carole," she said, "I don't think you've ever realized your and Starlight's full potential."

Carole couldn't believe what was happening. For more than a week she'd been living in agony simply because she wouldn't share her dilemma with anyone. Now, the minute she mentioned it, she saw a different side—a number of different sides. King wasn't her only chance for success. She and Starlight *could* go on to bigger and better things! Carole was so overwrought from rethinking the situation that she didn't trust herself to speak.

Fortunately, Pat Naughton filled in. "I'll bet I know what the announcement is. You wouldn't sell this boy in a million years, would you?"

Carole shook her head, her eyes shining. She clasped her arms around Starlight's neck and buried her face in his mane. "I—I just couldn't, Pat!" she cried.

Seeing Carole cry set Stevie and Lisa off, too. Pat shot

Mrs. Reg a curious glance as The Saddle Club bawled their heads off.

Finally, Carole raised her head and sniffed. "I sure am lucky you've been riding him, though, Pat. Otherwise riding for Max tomorrow would be frightening!"

Stevie and Lisa looked at one another. "Max!" they both cried.

"But—But you two are all set, aren't you?" Carole asked. "You've been riding every day, right?"

Stevie smiled weakly.

"Not exactly," Lisa began.

AN HOUR LATER the girls were sitting in the tack room, racking their brains.

"What if we tell Max there was a huge snowstorm and all the roads were closed and . . ." Stevie stopped. "Nah."

Carole sat forward. "How about this: The horses got into the grain room and colicked. They're all fine now, but . . ." She sighed. "Nah."

"How about . . ." said Lisa. "Nah."

"There's always bribery," Stevie suggested hopefully. "I've been baking a lot, and I could always whip up a batch of peanut butter cookies by tomorrow morning."

"Hey! You've got something!" Lisa said. "I'm almost

through with my needlepoint pattern. I could give it to Maxi or Deborah as a gift!"

"Gee, I don't have anything," Carole said.

"Yes you do!" said Stevie. "You can say your project was to help Pat find a horse as good as Starlight! It's not your fault it was an impossible task."

Carole looked doubtful. Then she started to giggle. Their predicament was truly awful, but just knowing the three of them were in it together made the whole thing seem a lot less worrisome.

Stevie giggled, too. "I'm really going to be in trouble with Max," she said. "By the time I get into the saddle, I'll be so tired from the competition with Alex I'll probably fall off! *With* stirrups, let alone without."

"Competition?" Carole asked.

Stevie described the showdown with Alex, as well as her preparations—jogging, the abs and arms video.

"That's it!" Lisa exclaimed.

"You figured out our demonstration for Max?" Stevie asked breathlessly.

"No. I figured out how you can beat Alex!"

"How?"

"No stirrups!"

"Huh?"

"Put in a no-stirrups phase of the competition!" Lisa explained. "You'll whip him there for sure."

116

"It's brilliant!" Stevie cried. "Alex won't know what hit him." They whooped it up for several minutes. Then they resumed their brooding silence.

"If only there were some way this fitness competition could help us with Max," Lisa mused.

"Careful," Carole warned her. "I haven't been working out at all. My abs and arms are just as wimpy as ever."

"Ha, ha! You're in the best *riding* shape of any of us," Stevie replied. "In fact, your abs and arms are probably stronger from riding and lugging tack and buckets around than—"

"Now, *that's* it!" Lisa shouted. This time she jumped up and did a little dance. "I just hope there's time. Why oh why didn't I think of this before?"

Carole and Stevie sat watching her. She ran out of the tack room and came back a moment later with a piece of paper. Using the stub of a pencil, she scribbled down a To Do list. "Come on," she said, observing her friends still sitting, "we've got to hurry. We don't have much light left. We'll have to do the taping indoors. Let's move! Let's put this grand plan into action, girls!"

"Uh, Lis'?" said Stevie.

"Yes?"

"Would you mind, ah, *telling* Carole and me what the grand plan *is*?"

Lisa looked from one to the other of them and burst

117

out laughing. "Gosh, you're demanding! The plan is this: We're going to make a video—a fitness video, just like the abs and arms one, only for riding."

"You mean we'll tape ourselves?" Stevie asked, marveling at Lisa's quick thinking.

Lisa nodded. "Yup. Doing all kinds of exercises, on the ground and on horseback. Among the three of us, we ought to be able to think up a video's worth."

"And we'll show it to Max in place of a demonstration!" Stevie cried, the light dawning.

"I've got some great ones," said Carole enthusiastically. "There's the stand-up-in-your-stirrups-and-touch-your-toes, there's the touch-the-horse's-ears-while—"

"No offense, Carole," said Lisa, "but save it for the video!"

The girls flew into action. Carole borrowed Mrs. Reg's video camera, the one that was normally used to record every second of Maxi's day. Stevie got dressed in boots and breeches to be the first demonstrator. And Lisa tacked up old, reliable Patch, the ideal horse to use in the mounted exercises.

When they met back in the indoor ring, Carole handed the video camera to Lisa. "You can start the taping," she said. "I just remembered something I have to do."

Carole went to Max's office. Mrs. Reg was inside. "Did you run out of videotape already?" she asked.

"No," said Carole. "I was wondering if I could use the phone."

"Of course, Carole, if it's important."

"It is," Carole assured her.

"I'll give you some privacy," the older woman said, standing up to leave.

As Carole dialed Jenny's number, something came back to her. With the phone to her ear, she leaned out the door. "Mrs. Reg? You know that dress you were telling me about? The one you made yourself?"

Mrs. Reg smiled. "What dress was that?" she asked innocently before disappearing down the aisle.

"I thought you said—!" Carole began. But Jenny picked up, and her sentence was left unfinished.

"Carole? Where are you? King and I have been waiting for you," Jenny said. "I thought you were going to bring the check by today."

"I can't," Carole said, her voice trembling. She took a deep breath. She knew from experience that it was better to get these awkward conversations over with as fast as possible.

"Would tomorrow work better for you?" Jenny asked.

For a moment Carole thought of King's big floating trot, of the feeling of sitting atop all that power, energy, and grace. But then she thought of soaring over a fence on Starlight's back. "No, I'm sorry. I'm not going to come back at all," Carole said hurriedly. "I've decided not to sell my horse. I'm sorry," she said again.

There was a long pause at the other end of the line. Finally Jenny said, "I thought you'd made the decision to concentrate on dressage. That's the only way to get to the top, you know."

Carole was still trembling, only now from anger more than fear. "I could get to the top jumping, too!" she retorted. Then she got control of herself. "I like dressage, but I don't want to give up jumping. Riding King was so great I forgot how much I love cross-country and show jumping."

"Well, it's your decision," Jenny said coldly.

As soon as she hung up, Carole felt as if the sky had suddenly lightened and she could see clearly. Jenny was no friend of hers! She was just a professional rider trying to sell a horse. Maybe she wasn't technically dishonest, but Carole didn't like the way she did business. Why hadn't she mentioned King's jumping problems?

Then Carole sighed. She could have figured out that King couldn't jump; she had, in fact, on two occasions— when he had tripped over the small fence in the ring (and she'd blamed herself) and when he had refused a jump out on the trail. The truth was she'd been so caught up in the idea of herself as a champion dressage rider that she had been blind to the horse's faults. On the other hand, with

Starlight she was overly critical because she knew him so well. So even when Pat was complimenting her, she couldn't hear the praise. It was that simple. Thinking of Mrs. Reg's story about the dress, Carole giggled. How on earth, she wondered, did Mrs. Reg always know?

ON THE LAST Saturday of her winter vacation, Stevie jumped out of bed at 6:40 A.M.: five minutes before her alarm went off. "I'm fit as a fiddle and feeling fine!" she hollered down the hall.

"Save it for later!" a voice yelled back. *Alex,* Stevie thought, grinning. And he sounded scared.

Clad in sweats and running shoes, Stevie trotted downstairs and wolfed a Power-Fitness bar. Her mother was in the kitchen making muffins and a big pot of coffee. "Refreshments for the spectators," she explained.

"Spectators?" Stevie asked.

Mrs. Lake nodded. "Yes, since you invited Carole and

Lisa, I invited their parents. So you should have a good turnout."

"Excellent! The more people to watch me whip Alex, the better!" Stevie said, though she felt a momentary attack of last-minute nerves.

A few minutes before seven, Carole drove up with Colonel Hanson, and Lisa and her parents walked over. While the parents drank coffee in the kitchen, Lisa put Stevie through her stretches and coached her on race strategy. "Let him set a fast pace if he wants to. Maybe it'll be too fast and he'll burn himself out."

At seven sharp, the two contestants strode out to the top of the driveway. Lisa made them shake hands, then announced, "This is an overall fitness competition between Stevie Lake and Alex Lake. It will consist of a three-mile race, a push-up and sit-up contest, and a third phase to take place at Pine Hollow Stables."

Alex looked surprised. "What third phase?"

"You'll see," Stevie replied nonchalantly.

"What are you going to do, make me jump an oxer?" Alex joked nervously.

Stevie looked her brother in the eye, unflinching. "May the best twin win," she said.

"They're off!" cried Stevie's father, the official timer. The two sprinted down the driveway, as evenly matched as could be, each one's stride mirroring the other's. Once they had disappeared from view, there was nothing to do but wait. Pat Naughton was stationed at an oak tree down the road that marked the turn-around point to make sure each of the Lakes tagged it. The parents went back inside, but Carole and Lisa leaned against the house, their fingers crossed for Stevie.

"So, are you sorry not to be buying the dressage horse?" Lisa asked. She could sense that Carole hadn't shared what a big decision she had faced.

Carole shook her head. Then she confessed, "Well, maybe the tiniest bit. He was incredible on the flat. But he'll be around. And there are other dressage horses if I ever do decide to specialize."

Lisa nodded. "It must be hard for you in a way," she said thoughtfully. "You're so talented, Carole, and you've done so much at such a young age. . . . I'll bet it's hard sometimes to know what comes next."

"It is—sometimes," admitted Carole, impressed and touched that Lisa could understand her situation so well. *But of course!* she thought. Lisa must feel like that in school, with academics, where she, too, was ahead of her years. Carole was about to say something when a shout went up from the kitchen window and the adults came pouring back out of the house. Someone had seen a flash of a windbreaker. The twins were drawing near!

124

A moment later they heard the sound of panting. Alex's head bobbed over the hedge, followed by Stevie's, not ten yards behind him. "Go for it, Stevie!" Lisa screamed. "Pour it on!"

Brother and sister raced up the driveway. Stevie gained an inch, then another inch. She was grinding him down. They were neck and neck. They sprinted past the crowd. In the same moment, Alex stopped dead in front of the house and Stevie tagged it. Both doubled over, holding their sides.

"Who won, Mom?" Stevie yelled between pants.

"Yeah, tell us!" Alex cried.

Mr. and Mrs. Lake looked at one another. It was impossible to declare the winner. "What do they call this in horse racing?" asked Stevie's mother.

"Photo finish!" Carole and Lisa yelled.

UNFORTUNATELY FOR STEVIE, things were a bit clearer in the next phase of the competition. She held her own in sit-ups, but long after her arms had collapsed, Alex kept pumping out the push-ups. Finally Stevie snapped at her brother to stop.

"Don't you want to see my one-handed push-ups?" he asked.

"Not till you see my two-handed throttle!" Stevie growled.

At the end of phase two, the adults dispersed and went to their cars. The Saddle Club had a quick huddle to go over their plan for the video demonstration. Stevie barely had time to change from sweats to jeans. Up in her room, she went automatically to the laundry pile in her closet, only to find an empty hamper. She smiled, remembering. All her laundry was clean because she hadn't been riding in so long. The funny thing was, she kind of missed the pile. Her room was too *neat* without it.

PINE HOLLOW WAS abuzz. Everyone was giving their horse a special grooming for Max's return. Pat was helping Carole with Starlight. "It's the least I can do," she said, wiping the bay's coat with a rag, "after your letting me ride him so much."

"Anytime, Pat," Carole said happily.

"Thanks," said Pat, "but as of next week, I'm going to have a whole lot less time for riding other people's horses. I've decided to buy the mare over in Pleasantville."

Carole thought back. "You mean the fifteen-year-old?" she asked.

"That's the one," said Pat, her voice full of enthusiasm. "I was worried about her age, and then I thought, 'Pat, you're just being silly.' Who knows where I'll be in three, four years, or what I'll want to do or if I'll even have the time to own a horse. She's a nice mare and I liked her from the beginning. Isn't it funny," she added, "how sometimes the perfect horse is right there the whole time and you don't notice?"

"It sure is," Carole said reflectively, running a comb through Starlight's forelock. "It sure is."

AFTER BRUSHING BELLE, Prancer, and Starlight, The Saddle Club met up in the tack room. "Thanks for keeping our tack shipshape," Lisa said to Carole.

"Yeah, it looks great," Stevie added.

Carole frowned. "I was going to thank you guys for the same thing. I haven't cleaned a piece of tack in two weeks!"

The girls were puzzled until Stevie suggested that maybe Red and Mrs. Reg had paid them back for all the work they had done over the years by secretly cleaning their tack.

"That must be it," said Carole. "We'll have to thank them."

"Better than thanks—I made peanut butter cookies last night," Stevie said.

"And I decided Maxi had enough gifts, so I'm giving the needlepoint I did to Mrs. Reg. She needlepoints herself, so she'll appreciate it," Lisa explained.

"Good," said Carole, hoisting her tack. "Then we're in the clear—at least with them. Max, I don't know about."

"You guys have nothing to worry about," Stevie complained. "Prancer and Starlight were ridden. Belle hasn't seen a bit since two Saturdays ago."

"Look on the bright side," Lisa advised her. "At least you'll look better than Veronica, breezing in from her ski vacation."

That thought perked Stevie up immediately.

THE GROUP OF horses and riders had just started their warm-up when Max strode into the indoor ring. He called them into the center. "I'm sorry I was delayed, but I've been looking around the stable areas. Thank you all so much for the hard work you put in while I was gone. It's obvious, and my mother and Red appreciated it enormously."

Stevie, Lisa, and Carole sank about a foot in their saddles.

"It was fun!" said Andrea Barry. "Wasn't it, Simon?"

"Sure was, Andrea," Simon replied. "Especially when we took apart the old carriage harness and oiled it from top to bottom."

Stevie, Lisa, and Carole felt their faces turning red.

"And when we cleaned out the hayloft to make room for the new load," Andrea said.

Just when The Saddle Club thought things couldn't get any worse, they did. The door of the indoor ring slid open and Veronica walked in. Or rather, she hobbled in, on crutches. "Skiing accident," she explained. "I twisted my ankle. Luckily I was able to fly home early and help with barn chores while you were gone, Max."

"So my mother told me," said Max, his voice appreciative. "She mentioned you'd been cleaning everyone's tack."

"Yes, well," Veronica said modestly, "not everyone's. Just the tack that wasn't getting used. Like Stevie's and Lisa's, and Carole's *saddle*—I couldn't do your bridle, Carole, because Pat used it when she was exercising Starlight."

The Saddle Club girls felt their blood begin to boil. "How dare she?" Stevie blurted out. "How dare she—"

"Clean your tack for you?" Max asked dryly. "Sounds like a major offense to me."

"But it's—it's not fair!" Stevie wailed.

"What's not?" asked Max, impatient.

"She can't get back at us by doing something *nice*. It doesn't work that way!"

Lisa and Carole didn't know whether to laugh or cry.

Veronica smiled sweetly. "It was the least I could do, Max. They've done so much for me."

Before Stevie could grab Veronica's crutches and whack her over the head with them, Max called the lesson to order. He told everyone to line up against the far side of the ring, dismount if they wanted, and watch the individual demonstrations.

Andrea went first. She said Doc had gotten lazy about his flying lead changes, so she had worked on those. She demonstrated several. Doc looked like the polished show horse he was.

"A good goal, well met," Max said. "It's focused and specific, and obviously your schooling worked."

Rejoining the group, Andrea looked flushed and happy.

Simon said Barq hadn't been paying enough attention to his aids. He had worked on transitions, backing up his leg aids with a crop if necessary to sharpen Barq's responsiveness. Max seemed pleased and told Simon to keep working on it.

"Next!"

"We three are together!" Lisa called.

Max gave them a look as if to say, "Big surprise there." "All right, get to it!" he ordered.

Stevie held the horses while Lisa and Carole ran out of the ring. A murmur went through the group. It got louder when the two returned wheeling the big-screen TV. Normally the TV was used only for riding clinics and horse shows; individuals would be taped and then could watch themselves and critique their performances.

"Hurry!" Lisa urged as Carole ran to connect the extension cord.

A small group had gathered in the spectator area: The Saddle Club parents plus Stevie's brothers, Pat Naughton, Red O'Malley, and Mrs. Reg. Deborah, carrying Maxi, joined them.

"Lights!" Lisa called.

Carole hit the lights, Lisa pressed Play, and the video started.

"Hello," said Lisa's voice-over. "This is a video that will teach you how to get in shape for riding. Some people think riding is not a real sport, that 'you just sit there and the horse does all the work.' Those who ride, however," she said ominously, "know better."

One by one, each of The Saddle Club girls appeared, demonstrating stretches, strengtheners, and basic limbering exercises. One exercise—Stevie appeared, hanging her heels off a step—would help you keep your heels down. Another—Carole was shown, picking up her shoulders and dropping them—would help you keep your shoulders down, back, and relaxed.

For the second half of the tape, Carole took over the voice narration as first Lisa, then Stevie, rode Patch while the other held the longe line. As Patch walked, trotted, and cantered, they repeated most of the exercises or variations of them in the saddle.

Watching the tape, the girls felt giddy with relief. The whole project had been so last-minute that anything could have happened. But except for a few rough transitions, the video looked good. When Carole switched the lights back on, there was a moment of silence. Then Max put his hands together. He clapped slowly three times. That seemed to be the cue for everyone to start clapping and talking.

"I'm throwing out my *Brand New Bod* video and using this one!" Deborah announced.

"Can we get copies?" asked Pat. "I hope we can get copies."

"What a great idea! I wish I had thought of it!" Andrea exclaimed.

"Too bad you didn't get really nice riding outfits," muttered Veronica. "It looks kind of backyard."

Any insult from Veronica meant one thing: jealousy. The Saddle Club high-fived in the middle of the ring. "We pulled it off!" Lisa whispered. "Somehow we pulled it off at the last minute!"

"Please," said Stevie, "my whole life is pulling things off at the last minute."

"Ahem." Max cleared his throat. "Am I correct in assuming that this takes the place of your mounted demonstrations?"

The Saddle Club nodded.

Max surveyed their horses carefully. Prancer was prancing at the end of her reins. Starlight couldn't seem to

132

stand still, either. And Belle was pawing madly at the turf and neighing from time to time. "They look a little high-strung," Max said finally. "Would you mind explaining that?"

Carole frowned. Lisa bit her lip. What could they say? How could they explain their two-week vacation from schooling their horses? Stevie stepped forward. "Max, remember how, before you left, you told us that horses could get barn fever? When they were cooped up and did too much of the same thing?"

Max nodded. "Ye-es," he said uncertainly.

"Well, it's easy," Stevie said. "We had horse fever!"

13

"THAT'S RIGHT," CAROLE said. "And now we're cured."

Max laughed long and heartily. "Fair enough," he said. "It happens to the best of us. Even, *ahem*, I went away for two weeks, in case you hadn't noticed."

When the TV was put away, Max suggested they all mount up and ride, doing whatever they liked. "Only don't take *too* long. Everyone's invited back to our house in an hour for doughnuts and cider straight from Vermont."

The lesson group cheered. "An hour?" Stevie said. "That's more than enough time. Oh, A-lex!"

In the seating area, Alex groaned. "Ready to 'just sit there' for twenty minutes?" Stevie asked gleefully. She mounted Belle and gave Alex his choice of Star-light or Prancer. He chose Prancer. Privately Carole was glad because it meant she could ride Starlight herself.

As it turned out, she needn't have worried. Alex lasted all of five minutes at the sitting trot *with* stirrups and two strides without. Stevie, meanwhile, felt she could have gone on forever. She could hardly believe it, but her fitness program had helped her riding. "I was wrong! Belle's trot isn't that bouncy at all. Poor thing! I blamed her when it was my fault!"

"Don't beat yourself up too much," said Carole. She reached down to give Starlight a pat. "The important thing is that The Saddle Club is back!"

WHEN EVERYONE HAD gathered at the Regnerys', Mr. and Mrs. Lake declared the fitness competition a tie. "Aw, Mom and Dad, you have to say that. You're our parents!" Stevie complained.

"No kidding!" Alex said. "Pretty lame judges, if you ask me!"

Max came in carrying a pot of hot cider. He set it down on a side table. "Hey, Lisa, I meant to tell you, I really liked that line at the beginning of the video, the one about how some people say 'you just sit there.' Whoever thinks that about riding is obviously—"

"Clueless?" Stevie interrupted, grinning at Alex. "I agree."

The Saddle Club was squeezed onto a small couch in the Regnerys' living room. On the opposite wall, there were lots of framed pictures—of horses, students, Max when he was little . . . All three girls happened to catch sight of one particular picture at the same time, and no wonder: It was of them!

"Hey!" said Stevie. "That's like the one I have, only it's more recent!"

"Yeah, you can tell by the horses," Carole said.

"Belle, Prancer, and Starlight," Lisa mused aloud. "Instead of Topside, Pepper, and Barq. Mrs. Reg?" she inquired. "When was that taken?"

"Not too long ago," said Mrs. Reg. "A few weeks at most—just using up some old film, you know. I've been meaning to give you girls the copies I had made, but it never seemed to be the right time."

There was a moment of silence as The Saddle Club took this in. "Would now be the right time?" Lisa asked hesitantly.

"Yes," Mrs. Reg said kindly. "I think it would."

While Mrs. Reg went to get the copies, the girls sat back against the couch, letting the conversation swirl around them. Each of them was lost in her own thoughts. Carole was thinking about how she couldn't wait to go home and write the story. Only now it was going to be about a girl who decided to keep her horse. And Carole knew exactly what she would say. She didn't care if she won the contest or if her English teacher gave her an A. The important thing was to write it. Maybe she could turn it into a novel and become an author of books about horses. That was one horsey career she'd never considered . . .

Lisa was thinking about a million things—whether Mrs. Reg would like the needlepoint; whether she'd be able to get her English homework done; whether she had mailed the thank-you note to Mrs. Chambers; how long it would take her mother to start complaining again about the amount of time she spent riding . . .

Stevie was thinking that technically she *had* beaten Alex because she had done more push-ups than he had done minutes of riding. "Oh, no!" she exclaimed, sitting up suddenly.

"What?" said Lisa and Carole.

"School starts Monday!"

"You're worried about not having enough time for homework and riding?" Lisa guessed.

"No." Stevie shook her head. "It's worse. I just realized I'm going to miss *Priced to Sell!*"

What happens to The Saddle Club next?
Read Bonnie Bryant's exciting new series
and find out.

High school. Driver's licenses. Boyfriends. Jobs.

A lot of new things are happening, but one thing
remains the same: Stevie Lake, Lisa Atwood, and Carole Hanson are still best friends. However, even among
best friends some things do change, and problems can
strain any friendship . . . but these three can handle
it. Can't they?

Read an excerpt from Pine Hollow #1: *The Long Ride*.

PROLOGUE

"Do you think we'll get there in time?" Stevie Lake asked, looking around for some reassuring sign that the airport was near.

"Since that plane almost landed on us, I think it's safe to say that we're close," Carole Hanson said.

"Turn right here," said Callie Forester from the backseat.

"And then left up ahead," Carole advised, picking out directions from the signs that flashed past near the airport entrance. "I think Lisa's plane is leaving from that terminal there."

"Which one?"

"The one we just passed," Callie said.

"Oh," said Stevie. She gripped the steering wheel tightly and looked for a way to turn around without causing a major traffic tie-up.

"This would be easier if we were on horseback," said Carole.

"Everything's easier on horseback," Stevie agreed.

"Or if we had a police escort," said Callie.

"Have you done that?" Stevie asked, trying to maneuver the car across three lanes of traffic.

"I have," said Callie. "It's kind of fun, but dangerous. It makes you think you're almost as important as other people tell you you are."

Stevie rolled her window down and waved wildly at the confused drivers around her. Clearly, her waving confused them more, but it worked. All traffic stopped. She crossed the necessary three lanes and pulled onto the service road.

It took another ten minutes to get back to the right and then ten more to find a parking place. Five minutes into the terminal. And then all that was left was to find Lisa.

"Where do you think she is?" Carole asked.

"I know," said Stevie. "Follow me."

"That's what we've been doing all morning," Callie said dryly. "And look how far it's gotten us."

But she followed anyway.

ALEX LAKE REACHED across the table in the airport cafeteria and took Lisa Atwood's hand.

"It's going to be a long summer," he said.

Lisa nodded. Saying good-bye was one of her least favorite activities. She didn't want Alex to know how hard it was, though. That would just make it tougher on him. The two of them had known each other for four years—as long as Lisa had been best friends with Alex's twin sister, Stevie. But they'd only started dating six months earlier. Lisa could hardly believe that. It seemed as if she'd been in love with him forever.

"But it is just for the summer," she said. The words sounded dumb even as they came out of her mouth. The summer *was* long. She wouldn't come back to Virginia until right before school started.

"I wish your dad didn't live so far away, and I wish the summer weren't so long."

"It'll go fast," said Lisa.

"For you, maybe. You'll be in California, surfing or something. I'll just be here, mowing lawns."

"I've never surfed in my life—"

"Until now," said Alex. It was almost a challenge, and Lisa didn't like it.

"I don't want to fight with you," said Lisa.

"I don't want to fight with you, either," he said, relenting. "I'm sorry. It's just that I want things to be different. Not very different. Just a little different."

"Me too," said Lisa. She squeezed his hand. It was a way to keep from saying anything else, because she was afraid that if she tried to speak she might cry, and she hated it when she cried. It made her face red and puffy, but most of all, it told other people how she was feeling. She'd found it useful to keep her feelings to herself these days. Like Alex, she wanted things to be different, but she wanted them to be very different, not just a little. She sighed. That was slightly better than crying.

"I TOLD YOU SO," said Stevie to Callie and Carole.

Stevie had threaded her way through the airport terminal, straight to the cafeteria near the security checkpoint. And there, sitting next to the door, were her twin brother and her best friend.

"Surprise!" the three girls cried, crowding around the table.

"We just couldn't let you be the only one to say goodbye to Lisa," Carole said, sliding into the booth next to Alex.

"We had to be here, too. You understand that, don't you?" Stevie asked Lisa as she sat down next to her.

"And since I was in the car, they brought me along," said Callie, pulling up a chair from a nearby table.

"You guys!" said Lisa, her face lighting up with joy. "I'm so glad you're here. I was afraid I wasn't going to see you for months and months!"

She *was* glad they were there. It wouldn't have felt right if she'd had to leave without seeing them one more time. "I thought you had other things to do."

"We just told you that so we could surprise you. We did surprise you, didn't we?"

"You surprised me," Lisa said, beaming.

"Me too," Alex said dryly. "I'm surprised, too. I really thought I could go for an afternoon, just *one* afternoon of my life, without seeing my twin sister."

Stevie grinned. "Well, there's always tomorrow," she said. "And that's something to look forward to, right?"

"Right," he said, grinning back.

Since she was closest to the outside, Callie went and got sodas for herself, Stevie, and Carole. When she rejoined the group, they were talking about everything in the world except the fact that Lisa was going to be gone for the summer and how much they were all going to miss one another.

She passed the drinks around and sat quietly at the end of the table. There wasn't much for her to say. She didn't really feel as if she belonged there. She wasn't anybody's best friend. It wasn't as if they minded her being there, but she'd come along because Stevie had offered to drive her to a tack shop after they left the airport. She was simply along for the ride.

". . . And don't forget to say hello to Skye."

"Skye? Skye who?" asked Alex.

"Don't pay any attention to him," Lisa said. "He's just jealous."

"You mean because Skye is a movie star?"

"And say hi to your father and the new baby. It must be exciting that you'll meet your sister."

"Well, of course, you've already met her, but now she's crawling, right? It's a whole different thing."

An announcement over the PA system brought their chatter to a sudden halt.

"It's my flight," Lisa said slowly. "They're starting to board and I've got to get through security and then to Gate . . . whatever."

"Fourteen," Alex said. "It comes after Gate Twelve. There are no thirteens in airports."

"Let's go."

"Here, I'll carry that."

"And I'll get this one . . ."

As Callie watched, Lisa hugged Carole and Stevie. Then she kissed Alex. Then she hugged her friends again. Then she turned to Alex.

"I think it's time for us to go," Carole said tactfully.

"Write or call every day," Stevie said.

"It's a promise," said Lisa. "Thanks for coming to the airport. You, too, Callie."

Callie smiled and gave Lisa a quick hug before all the girls backed off from Lisa and Alex.

Lisa waved. Her friends waved and turned to leave her alone with Alex. They were all going to miss her, but the girls had one another. Alex only had his lawns to mow. He needed the last minutes with Lisa

"See you at home!" Stevie called over her shoulder, but she didn't think Alex heard. His attention was completely focused on one person.

Carole wiped a tear from her eye once they'd rounded a corner. "I'm going to miss her."

"Me too," said Stevie.

Carole turned to Callie. "It must be hard for you to understand," she said.

"Not really," said Callie. "I can tell you three are really close."

"We are," Carole said. "Best friends for a long time. We're practically inseparable." Even to her the words sounded exclusive and uninviting. If Callie noticed, she didn't say anything.

The three girls walked out of the terminal and found their way to Stevie's car. As she turned on the engine, Stevie was aware of an uncomfortable empty feeling. She really didn't like the idea of Lisa's being gone for the summer, and her own unhappiness was not going to be helped by a brother who was going to spend the entire time moping about his missing girlfriend. There had to be something that would make her feel better.

"Say, Carole, do you want to come along with us to the tack shop?" she asked.

"No, I can't," Carole said. "I promised I'd bring in the horses from the paddock before dark, so you can just drop me off at Pine Hollow. Anyway, aren't you due at work in an hour?"

Stevie glanced at her watch. Carole was right. Everything was taking longer than it was supposed to this afternoon.

"Don't worry," Callie said quickly. "We can go to the tack shop another time."

"You don't mind?" Stevie asked.

"No. I don't. Really," said Callie. "I don't want you to be late for work—either of you. If my parents decide to get a pizza for dinner again, I'm going to want it to arrive on time!"

Stevie laughed, but not because she thought anything was very funny. She wasn't about to forget the last time she'd delivered a pizza to Callie's family. In fact, she wished it hadn't happened, but it had. Now she had to find a way to face up to it.

As she pulled out of the airport parking lot, a plane roared overhead, rising into the brooding sky. *Maybe that's Lisa's plane*, she thought. The noise of its flight seemed to mark the beginning of a long summer.

The first splats of rain hit the windshield as Stevie paid their way out of the parking lot. By the time they were on the highway, it was raining hard. The sky had darkened to a steely gray. Streaks of lightning brightened it, only to be followed by thunder that made the girls jump.

The storm had come out of nowhere. Stevie flicked on the windshield wipers and hoped it would go right back to nowhere.

The sky turned almost black as the storm strengthened.

Curtains of rain ripped across the windshield, pounding on the hood and roof of the car. The wipers flicked uselessly at the torrent.

"I hope Fez is okay," said Callie. "He hates thunder, you know."

"I'm not surprised," said Carole, trying to control her voice. It seemed to her that there were a lot of things Fez hated. He was as temperamental as any horse she had ever ridden.

Fez was one of the horses in the paddock. Carole didn't want to upset Callie by telling her that. If she told Callie he'd been turned out, Callie would wonder why he hadn't just been exercised. If she told Callie she'd exercised him, Callie might wonder if he was being overworked. Carole shook her head. What was it about this girl that made Carole so certain that whatever she said, it would be wrong? Why couldn't she say the one thing she really needed to say?

Still, Carole worked at Pine Hollow, and that meant taking care of the horses that were boarding there—and that meant keeping the owners happy.

"I'm sure Fez will be fine. Ben and Max will look after him," Carole said.

"I guess you're right," said Callie. "I know he can be difficult. Of course, you've ridden him, so you know that, too. I mean, that's obvious. But it's spirit, you see. Spirit is the key to an endurance specialist. He's got it, and I think he's got the makings of a champion. We'll work together this summer, and come fall . . . well, you'll see."

Spirit—yes, it was important in a horse. Carole knew

that. She just wished she understood why it was that Fez's spirit was so irritating to her. She'd always thought of herself as someone who'd never met a horse she didn't like. Maybe it was the horse's owner . . .

"Uh-oh," said Stevie, putting her foot gently on the brake. "I think I got it going a little too fast there."

"You've got to watch out for that," Callie said. "My father says the police practically lie in wait for teenage drivers. They love to give us tickets. Well, they certainly had fun with me."

"You got a ticket?" Stevie asked.

"No, I just got a warning, but it was almost worse than a ticket. I was going four miles over the speed limit in our hometown. The policeman stopped me, and when he saw who I was, he just gave me a warning. Dad was furious—at me and at the officer, though he didn't say anything to the officer. He was angry at him because he thought someone would find out and say I'd gotten special treatment! I was only going four miles over the speed limit. Really. Even the officer said that. Well, it would have been easier if I'd gotten a ticket. Instead, I got grounded. Dad won't let me drive for three months. Of course, that's nothing compared to what happened to Scott last year."

"What happened to Scott?" Carole asked, suddenly curious about the driving challenges of the Forester children.

"Well, it's kind of a long story," said Callie. "But—"

"Wow! Look at that!" Stevie interrupted. There was an amazing streak of lightning over the road ahead. The dark afternoon brightened for a minute. Thunder followed instantly.

"Maybe we should pull off the road or something?" Carole suggested.

"I don't think so," said Stevie. She squinted through the windshield. "It's not going to last long. It never does when it rains this hard. We get off at the next exit anyway."

She slowed down some more and turned the wipers up a notch. She followed the car in front of her, keeping a constant eye on the two red spots of the car's taillights. She'd be okay as long as she could see them. The rain pelted the car so loudly that it was hard to talk. Stevie drove on cautiously.

Then, as suddenly as it had started, the rain stopped. Stevie spotted the sign for their exit, signaled, and pulled off to the right and up the ramp. She took a left onto the overpass and followed the road toward Willow Creek.

The sky was as dark as it had been, and there were clues that there had been some rain there, but nothing nearly as hard as the rain they'd left on the interstate. Stevie sighed with relief and switched the windshield wipers to a slower rate.

"I think I'll drop you off at Pine Hollow first," she said, turning onto the road that bordered the stable's property.

Pine Hollow's white fences followed the contour of the road, breaking the open, grassy hillside into a sequence of paddocks and fields. A few horses stood in the fields, swishing their tails. One bucked playfully and ran up a hill, shaking his head to free his mane in the wind. Stevie smiled. Horses always seemed to her the most welcoming sight in the world.

"Then I'll take Callie home," Stevie continued, "and

after that I'll go over to Pizza Manor. I may be a few minutes late for work, but who orders pizza at five o'clock in the afternoon anyway?"

"Now, now," teased Carole. "Is that any way for you to mind your Pizza Manors?"

"Well, at least I have my hat with me," said Stevie. Or did she? She looked into the rearview mirror to see if she could spot it, and when that didn't do any good, she glanced over her shoulder. Callie picked it up and started to hand it to her.

"Here," she said. "We wouldn't want— Wow! I guess the storm isn't over yet!"

The sky had suddenly filled with a brilliant streak of lightning, jagged and pulsating, accompanied by an explosion of thunder.

It startled Stevie. She shrieked and turned her face back to the road. The light was so sudden and so bright that it blinded her for a second. The car swerved. Stevie braked. She clutched at the steering wheel and then realized she couldn't see because the rain was pelting even harder than before. She reached for the wiper control, switching it to its fastest speed.

There was something to her right! She saw something move, but she didn't know what it was.

"Stevie!" Carole cried.

"Look out!" Callie screamed from the backseat.

Stevie swerved to the left on the narrow road, hoping it would be enough. Her answer was a sickening jolt as the car slammed into something solid. The car spun around, smashing against the thing again. When the thing screamed, Stevie knew it was a horse. Then it disappeared from her field of vision. Once again, the car spun. It smashed against the guardrail on the left side of the road and tumbled up and over it as if the rail had never been there.

Down they went, rolling, spinning. Stevie could hear the screams of her friends. She could hear her own voice, echoing in the close confines of the car, answered by the thumps of the car rolling down the hillside into a gully. Suddenly the thumping stopped. The screams were stilled. The engine cut off. The wheels stopped spinning. And all Stevie could hear was the idle *slap, slap, slap* of her windshield wipers.

"Carole?" she whispered. "Are you okay?"

"I think so. What about you?" Carole answered.

"Me too. Callie? Are you okay?" Stevie asked.

There was no answer.

"Callie?" Carole echoed.

The only response was the girl's shallow breathing.

How could this have happened?

ABOUT THE AUTHOR

Bonnie Bryant is the author of nearly a hundred books about horses, including The Saddle Club series, Saddle Club Super Editions, and the Pony Tails series. She has also written novels and movie novelizations under her married name, B. B. Hiller.

Ms. Bryant began writing The Saddle Club in 1986. Although she had done some riding before that, she intensified her studies then and found herself learning right along with her characters Stevie, Carole, and Lisa. She claims that they are all much better riders than she is.

Ms. Bryant was born and raised in New York City. She still lives there, in Greenwich Village, with her two sons.

Don't miss the next exciting
Saddle Club adventure . . .

SECRET HORSE
Saddle Club #86

The Saddle Club has a secret!

Stevie Lake, Carole Hanson, and Lisa Atwood are hoping to compete in a prestigious horse show. To that end, they're doing everything they can to stay on stable owner Max Regnery's good side—including doing extra chores around Pine Hollow, such as exercising stable horses like Samson.

Veronica diAngelo is sure she'll be making the trip to the horse show—just as she's sure she'll bring home a blue ribbon. And of course Veronica has no intention of lifting a finger to help anyone.

The Saddle Club would love to beat Veronica, but how? She and her horse are tough competition. Then Lisa takes Samson over a jump. He's a natural. Now the Saddle Club has to keep their secret weapon under wraps and teach Veronica a lesson she won't forget!